Riddle Gully Runaway

For Nan and Pa who lived down the road
and whose arms were always wide open

First published 2014 by FREMANTLE PRESS
25 Quarry Street, Fremantle, Western Australia 6160
www.fremantlepress.com.au

Printed by Everbest Printing Company, China
Cover design and illustration by traceygibbs.com

National Library of Australia Cataloguing-in-publication entry
Banyard, Jen, 1958-
Riddle Gully Runaway/ Jen Banyard.
ISBN 978 1922 089 87 8 (pbk.)
A823.3

 Government of **Western Australia**
Department of **Culture and the Arts**

Fremantle Press is supported by the State Government
through the Department of Culture and the Arts.

Riddle Gully Runaway

Jen Banyard

 FREMANTLE PRESS

'If you master others, you are forceful.
If you master yourself, you have inner strength.'
Lao Tzu (6th century BCE), China

CHAPTER ONE

Someone had said the view from the top of the rollercoaster was amazing but Will Hopkins had only one thought as the carriage rattled its way up the steep steel incline: 'I'm only thirteen! I'm too young to die!'

Beside him in the lead car, Pollo di Nozi strained against the safety bar, pointing excitedly. 'Would you look at that bolt there, Will! It's wobbling like crazy! This rig needs a good going over with a welding torch if you ask me! There's another loose one! Look!'

Will stared ahead, across the treetops and the Riddle Gully fairground to the clock tower of the town hall in the distance. His eyes were like golf balls. His knuckles, as they gripped the bar, looked like eight snow-capped mountain-tops. Why had he ever listened to Pollo? Didn't he know that what Pollo called fun most often nearly killed him?

Crick-et-y ... crick-et-y ... crick-et-y ... He could hear each cog ratcheting into place, hauling them slowly upward to the crest. Will slid his eyeballs sideways and down and spotted Mr Wrigley, Riddle Gully's oldest mechanic, at the rollercoaster controls. He was shading his eyes and looking up at them. His bottom lip was jutting in a worried pout, Will was sure.

Crick-et-y ... crick-et-y ... Will gulped down the rising lump in his throat.

Pollo jabbed him with her elbow. 'Take a chill pill, Will! No one ever dies up here on these things.' She pointed to the ground below. 'They all die *down there*! In the dirt! Splat! Ha-ha-ha-ha-ha-ha-ha!'

Crick-et-y ... Their carriage inched to the crest of the iron-girder mountain. Will saw dotted farms and distant hills, lumpy with trees that looked much nicer from the ground. He saw the steely blue sky stretching around them — perfect if you were an albatross. He felt his heart hammer against his ribcage. The carriage teetered at the peak.

'Here we go!' yelled Pollo. 'The fun's about to ... Whoa-aa-aah!'

Slowly, irrevocably, they tipped. Suddenly, Will

and Pollo were hurtling into a bone-shaking plummet toward earth. Down they flew, their bodies pressed back by centrifugal force or terror — Will couldn't tell which. The car juddered on the narrow rail, sending tremors through their insides, down their limbs to their fingers and toes. Will's teeth jangled and his mouth gaped, but just a terrified squeeze of air, a scream so high-pitched only dogs could hear it, escaped. Beside him, Pollo let go of the bar, threw both arms in the air and hooted like a banshee.

No sooner had they bottomed out than the car swung hard right, throwing Will against Pollo. He was still trying to spit Pollo's long springy hair from his mouth when it swung hard left, flinging Pollo his way, bringing their heads together with a clunk. The tinny taste of blood filled Will's mouth and his tongue began to sting.

Will could see it up ahead — the twenty metre high, gravity-defying Loop of Extinction the rollercoaster was named for — looming against the sky. Ten minutes earlier he and Pollo had laughed at the terror on the upside-down faces of the passengers, their hair flying beneath their heads, their pleading screams as they hurtled around the loop. Now Pollo and Will flew at it headlong, their car rocking side to side.

They whizzed upwards. The passengers shrieked as a single organism. For a second, Will saw the gleaming steel rollercoaster rail below — then they whipped downwards. As Will's insides were catching up with the rest of him, they rocketed into an S-bend — right, left, right — to the groans and squeals of the riders behind. They missiled toward the string of tattered flags that marked the finish. Then, as violently as it had all begun, invisible hooks grabbed their carriage and yanked them to a dead stop.

A lanky teenaged attendant, his baseball cap angled over an ear, leaned across and unlatched the bars. He offered a steadying hand. Pollo didn't seem to notice it and sprang unaided onto the platform.

'That was insane!' she screeched. 'Let's go again!' She hurried toward the exit steps, shouting over her shoulder, 'I'll pay for you, Will, if you've run out of money!'

The attendant hauled Will from the car and gave him a nudge. But Will remained rooted to the spot, his legs wobbling like jelly-snakes, the mob pushing past either side. He stared like a zombie, his mouth hanging open, at the attendant's chest as though hypnotised by the image on his black T-shirt.

'Ee-yew, Will! You don't look so good.' Pollo was making her way back along the platform to her friend. Will's skin had taken on the colour of boiled cabbage.

The ride attendant unplugged music earphones and jerked his head toward the exit. 'Move along, please, buddy.' Pushing a *tss-tss-tss-tss* cymbal sound through his teeth and dipping his head to the beat, he shrugged and took Will by the armpits. Pollo alongside, he eased Will along the platform and down the metal steps onto the grass thoroughfare, Will's feet trailing unhelpfully.

'Take it easy, eh?' said the attendant, plugging in his earphones and springing back up the steps for the next round of victims.

Will stood on the pathway, swaying, with the crowd at the Riddle Gully annual fair snaking around him and Pollo. He tried to breathe deeply, tried to focus on something other than his squirming insides.

'Gee Will,' said Pollo. 'I've heard of people going green before but I've never actually seen it. I've gotta get a picture!' She pulled her camera from her pocket and snapped before Will could summon the strength to duck.

'You'd better not put that in your newspaper column,' he mumbled.

'Don't worry, my friend. My section of the *Coast* is only ever black and white. You're safe. I'm saving the embarrassing photo spot for Mayor Bullock. Why stop this year, eh?'

Two youths eating hotdogs, with fried onions and pus-like mustard sliding down their fingers, stopped to gawk. 'Watch out!' one laughed. 'This one's gonna blow!' They were rocking together, pointing at Will and sniggering, when, with the same suddenness the rollercoaster ride had come to an end, everything Will had eaten at the Riddle Gully fair that afternoon — the hamburger-with-egg, sour cream wedges, chocolate muffin, corn dog, two doughnuts and large blueberry slushy — rocketed up his throat and propelled themselves in a colourful arc towards the boys' feet.

Pollo clapped a hand to her mouth. The youths gazed from their spattered shoes to Will and back again. Both looked like they wanted to beat him up on the spot but were too disgusted to go near him. They stalked away, muttering and swearing, hurling their hotdogs onto the path. Two ravens flew down and began stabbing at the pink meat, hopping back and forth as pedestrians passed.

Will looked at Pollo sheepishly. 'Whew! I didn't feel it coming till the last second.'

'Well it's not like you're a giraffe or anything.'

'Huh?'

'A giraffe ... You know, with a mile-long neck. A giraffe would know something was coming. I wonder how long it takes a giraffe to throw up.'

'Maybe they never do, maybe the gunk never reaches the top,' said Will. 'That'd be neat.'

'I'll have to ask Dad. He'll know.'

'Handy having a vet for a dad sometimes.'

'Not as handy as you having a police sergeant for a stepdad. That would be brilliant in my line of work! I could get the scoop on Riddle Gully every night over dinner.'

'It has its ups and downs,' said Will. 'HB has this way of getting details out of me before I even know what we're talking about. Like the time he —'

From the corner of her eye, Pollo could see the rollercoaster attendant, his hi-top sneakers planted wide as he trickled sand from a bucket over Will's offering. He seemed to be taking extraordinary care over it. His head was tilted towards them and his earphones dangled loose from the pocket of his baggy jeans. Was he eavesdropping on them, wondered Pollo. Getting the low-down on the local arm of the law?

She put a hand on Will's shoulder. 'Say, let's head over to the Kitchens Rule tent. They've got free samples.'

'Good idea!' said Will, his face back to its usual pink. 'I'm hungry all over again now.'

CHAPTER TWO

They ambled in the spring sunshine away from the rollercoaster across the Riddle Gully fairground — a stretch of playing fields ringed by tall, dark Norfolk Island Pines that at the end of each winter, as soon as finals were over, was spruced up for the District Fair.

'My editor needs a report on the fair and I want to do something really special,' said Pollo. Her after-school cadetship as Youth Reporter for the *Coast* regional news network kept Riddle Gully on its toes; it also kept shiny Pollo's dream of becoming a professional investigative journalist like her mum had been. She ran her fingers down the leather thong around her neck to the notepad and pencil tied at the end. 'I'm going to buttonhole the judges in the Pickles and Chutneys Division and get the dirt on why Mayor Bullock wins it every year. There's funny business going on there, Will, and my readers would love to know what it is, I'm sure.'

They dodged toddlers in strollers, gooey ice-cream puddles and whirligigs on sticks, Pollo taking photos and jotting notes in her pad. People from all across the farming district milled. Adults ran into old friends and sugar-loaded kids zimmed like flying beetles between their legs. Tinny music pumped from competing portable sound systems and the smell of sizzling onions wafted on the air. Everyone was excited and happy, wandering the gritty trails between stalls and exhibits, their arms loaded with neon-pink stuffed prizes, second-hand treasures, or cling-wrapped trays of lumpy home-baked goodies.

The rollercoaster was new this year. Someone on the organising committee knew someone in the district Chamber of Commerce who had a cousin who had a friend who owed them a favour ... and hadn't opened a safety manual since the nineteen-sixties, thought Pollo, remembering those rickety bolts. She jotted a note in her pad to follow it up. There could be a story in it.

Pollo and Will stopped at the fairy floss van and each bought a stick.

'The guy at the rollercoaster,' said Will. 'Do you know him?'

'Who? Mr Wrigley?' said Pollo, lifting a sugary blue wisp and dangling it onto her tongue.

'No, the helper with the black T-shirt.'

'Aah! The rollercoaster kid! With the sideways cap! He looks like a breakdancer from the city who's lost his way. I was about to ask if *you* knew him,' said Pollo. 'I think he was listening in on us earlier. He's shady, if you ask me.'

'It's weird,' said Will. 'I've got this feeling I've seen him before. First I thought he came with the crew who put up the rollercoaster 'cos I saw Mayor Bullock yelling at him. Then I saw the logo for that hip-hop group Twisted Lips on his T-shirt and it rang a bell from somewhere. It's a rip-off of a Picasso painting we did at art school called *The Weeping Woman*. Face all over the place. It's probably why I threw up.'

Pollo drummed her fingertips against her chin. 'Mayor Bullock, you say? I wonder if he could be the nephew, Benson Bragg, who's come to stay with him and old Mrs Bullock. It would figure, from what I've heard about this nephew of his.'

'No way!' said Will, withdrawing his face from a puff

of purple floss. 'Mayor Bullock's nephew? The mayor's way too stuffy to be that kid's uncle. And as for inviting him to stay ...' He tore off some floss and lowered it into his mouth.

'Aah, but he didn't, you see. Old Mrs Bullock was in Sherri's second-hand shop the other day and told Sherri all about it. This Benson kid — her grandson, the mayor's nephew — was suspended from school. But then his mother — the mayor's sister — broke her leg and had to go to hospital. And his dad's away on work. So Benson's staying with them and the mayor is spitting chips!'

'Hah!' Will laughed. 'Mayor Bullock hates the youth of today, as he calls us — even nerdy kids like you! He's had it coming.' He waited for some people to pass and whispered, 'Did Mrs Bullock say *why* Benson was suspended?'

Pollo leaned close. 'Stealing! She let it slip. She thought it would be lovely having her grandson to stay with them, even so. But it's not working out like she hoped. The mayor wants to sort out his nephew with good old-fashioned discipline, as he puts it. Sherri reckons that's rich because the mayor never had any discipline himself, his mum and dad were such softies. I wonder what turns some people so mean?'

'I reckon sometimes they just don't try hard enough,' said Will. He pushed a hank of fairy floss into his mouth with a finger. 'It's dead easy to be a grouch, in my book. But getting along with people, even if you've got your own worries and stuff going on — that's heaps more effort.'

'Yeah, look at you!' said Pollo. 'Since you got busted for the graffiti last summer and had to do that course on dealing with anger, you haven't blown up once.'

'Jeepers! I never ever want to dig a hole for myself like that again! It's funny ... the longer I go without losing it the easier it gets. It's like I'm getting into the *habit* of being someone who keeps their cool.'

'Just like Mayor Bullock's in the habit of being a puffed-up pompous grump!' laughed Pollo. She checked her watch. 'Yikes! Speaking of Mayor Bullock, we'd better walk faster. I need to get my story on him, then get home and spruce up Shorn Connery for the Best Dressed Pet parade.'

'When is it?' asked Will.

'Five o'clock. The grand finale! Shorn Connery can't wait.'

Will frowned. 'How can you tell that a sheep can't wait?'

Pollo tutted. 'A supersleuth with finely tuned instincts like me just senses these things, blockhead! Besides, Shorn Connery and I have a special connection. You must know that by now!'

'Yeah, of course I do,' said Will, looking away to hide his smile.

*

They reached the Kitchens Rule tent. Before going in, Pollo aimed her camera at an elderly couple in striped jesters' hats, strolling arm in arm. 'For the record, whatever it was that Benson Bragg took,' she said from behind the lens, 'Sherri didn't seem to think it was serious.'

'But it was still stealing,' said Will.

'Yeah, I guess so,' said Pollo.

'Hmm ... I wonder ...'

Pollo lowered the camera and looked at Will. He carefully scraped the last bits of fairy floss off its stick with his fingernail, walked to a rubbish bin and dropped it in. When he turned back, Pollo's eyes were boring into him and her hands were on her hips.

'You wonder *what*? Are you going to tell me or not?'

Will looked at the passing parade of happy townspeople and farmers. No one seemed to be paying them much attention. 'D'you know when this Benson kid arrived in Riddle Gully?' he asked, his voice low.

'A week or so ago, I think. Why?'

'Hmm ...'

'Will Hopkins, you know something, don't you?' Pollo smiled pleasantly at Will. 'And you also know I'll bust your head in if you don't tell me!'

'We shouldn't go jumping to conclusions,' said Will.

'I've told you before,' Pollo hissed. 'Drawing conclusions and jumping to conclusions are entirely different things! Just give me the facts and I'll make up my own mind. I have good instincts in these matters. I *am* Youth Reporter —'

'— for the *Coast* news network,' Will finished. 'I know.'

Pollo huffed. 'I want justice and equality for all humankind, Will. And for that I need to give my readers the truth!'

'And juicy news stories,' added Will.

'Well, yes ... that's understood.' Pollo folded her arms and began tapping her foot, glaring at Will.

Will sighed and wished he'd kept his big mouth shut. It was useless. Pollo would bug him until he caved. He may as well get it over with. 'HB was talking to Angela last night in the kitchen,' he began. He stopped to wave heartily at a mate from school, hoping he'd veer their way. The boy grinned and waved back but, pointing to the phone at his ear, kept walking. Will turned back to Pollo whose eyes were now steely blades.

'Police Sergeant Talks to Wife in Kitchen,' she huffed. 'I can see the headline now! What did he *say* to your mum, Will?'

'I wasn't meant to be listening,' said Will.

'Excellent!' said Pollo. 'Go on!'

'Well, I overheard HB saying how there'd been a funny spate of little things disappearing lately. Rings and watches and stuff. Some of it had been reported at the station, but then at the tennis club yesterday people were talking. It turns out there's a lot more that hasn't been reported. Seems like Riddle Gully either has a petty thief on the loose, or something is making people very forgetful about where they put things.'

'A thief!' whispered Pollo.

'Or a coincidental string of people misplacing things,' cautioned Will. 'Or things could've gone missing ages ago — and it's only when people hear about the other stuff gone missing that they notice. That's what HB reckons has happened.'

'That explains it!' said Pollo.

'Yeah, well, it makes sense,' said Will.

'No! I mean, that explains Aunty Giulia's missing ring! She put it on a fence-post while she was moving rocks in the garden and it disappeared. It belonged to Grandma di Nozi. Old gold and emerald. Aunty Giulia's devastated.' Pollo stroked an invisible beard. 'And all these things vanish just as Mayor Bullock's nephew, a notorious purloiner of other people's property, comes to Riddle Gully. It's a pretty big coincidence, wouldn't you say?'

'It looks incriminating, I admit,' said Will.

'Incriminating! Hah! When you put together what you know and what I know, it's virtual proof Benson Bragg is at the bottom of all this. And if some pasty nephew of Mayor Bullock thinks he can waltz into Riddle Gully and start helping himself to people's valuables, he's got another think coming!'

'Keep your voice down, will you?' said Will, his head pivoting. 'Everyone can hear — and you haven't got a crumb of proof.'

Pollo put her face close to Will's and grinned. 'That's where you come in!'

'Don't look at me!' protested Will. 'I've told you enough already!'

Pollo ignored him. 'You just need to wheedle a teeny-tiny bit more info out of HB and we can put the squeeze on Benson Bragg. If he's anything like his uncle, he'll turn to jelly under pressure.'

'Oh no, Pollo!' The sick feeling from the rollercoaster began to squirm in Will all over again.

'Oh yes, Will! I'm going to turn you into an assistant supersleuth if it kills me!' She clapped her friend on the shoulder. 'I can feel a story coming on!'

Will slumped. 'I was afraid you'd say that.'

CHAPTER THREE

The flaking paint and rust of the fairground stalls had turned a soft gold in the mellowing light. Pollo, stomping along the main thoroughfare, didn't notice. Not only had she failed to get her story on the mayor and his chutney-swindle but she was late for the Best Dressed Pet parade. They had to get across to the far side of the fairground and her not-so-faithful assistant Shorn Connery was stopping every two seconds to snuffle at each gooey lolly and squashed chip along the grassy path. Hurrying him was futile. It was like he was *trying* to thwart her.

'You're going to bust out of that jacket if you don't stop eating!' Pollo tugged on his lead. The handsome costume she and Sherri had made for him — the top half of the dinner suit favoured by his namesake Sean Connery in his famous role as James Bond, Secret Agent 007 — was covered in flecks of dead grass and dobs of Shorn Connery's sticky spittle. She needed more time, not less, before the parade to clean him up and snaffle that first-prize cheque.

She tugged on the lead again. But Shorn Connery had found half a corn-dog this time and wasn't going anywhere. He flicked his stiff, white lashes and glared at Pollo. *Baa-aa-aah!*

Pollo was pretty sure that was ram-talk for 'The more you hurry me, the longer I'll take.'

Just then she had a brainwave. As soon as Shorn Connery was done with the corn-dog, she'd steer him off the main path to the back way — further to walk but quicker for sure.

Two minutes later Pollo and Shorn Connery were making good progress behind the tents and vans. They had just rounded a bend when Pollo spotted a lanky figure on his hands and knees, the toes of his hi-tops digging into the grass. He was peering beneath the canvas back wall of a tent — the white elephant stall if Pollo wasn't mistaken. The rollercoaster kid! Benson Bragg! Pollo glowered. Most of the stall owners kept their money up against the back wall of their tent — and here was the nephew of Riddle Gully's self-righteous mayor helping himself to it!

She whipped her camera from her pocket and took a photo. At the beep of the shutter, Benson swung around. He saw Pollo and with a quick twist flopped down on his backside — as though he was just a worker taking a break in the shade. He plugged in his earphone buds and began bobbing his head in time to the music.

Pollo kept her eyes fixed on him as she and Shorn Connery passed. Benson swivelled his cap around and tugged it low over his eyes. It's too late for that, thought Pollo, her eyes narrowed. She had Benson Bragg digitally nicked.

*

As they neared the marshalling yard for the Best Dressed Pet parade, Pollo saw the mob gathered. She tried to ignore the tightening sensation in her throat. There were heaps of people — three or four deep behind the rope fence with its little orange flags. Some of the adults had spent a little too long at the wine-tasting tent, by the look of them. Would Shorn Connery behave himself? He was strong, even for a ram ... and he wasn't used to crowds.

Two ravens shuffled on the lip of a rubbish bin, their glossy greenish-black throat hackles ruffling in the breeze. One with a small feather angling from its shoulder clamped a fragment of frayed rope in its beak, perhaps for a nest. The other gave a loud, flat caw as they passed. *Arp-arp-aaah!* The cry was almost pitying, thought Pollo, as though Shorn Connery had come last already.

Shorn Connery looked at them from rolled-back eyes and quickened his pace. He wasn't keen on ravens, Pollo knew. They liked to line their nests with his wool, freshly plucked. And he'd seen them pecking the eyes from his fallen comrades on Aunty Giulia and Uncle Pete's farm. That can't have helped. She hoped the birds wouldn't make him skittish here.

Pollo found the registration table and signed up. Behind her, she heard the crisp voice of the high school principal, Ms Piggott, the chief judge and referee. She was wearing a wide straw hat resplendent with silk daisies and was bending down to a boy of about seven whose eyes brimmed with tears. 'I'm sorry, Rooster, but I can't let you enter. Your carp may well have been alive when you painted it to look like a shark, but it's not anymore. It's in the rules. All contestants must be alive.

Look at your fish, lad. It's floating on the surface.'

'But that's how he swims, Miss! He always does that!'

At that moment, Rooster's father strode across. He dropped to one knee and spoke to his son, then looked up to Principal Piggott apologetically. 'I'm sorry, Principal, the wife and I didn't know about all this,' he said, and led the sniffling boy away.

Owners and pets were called to the parade ring. Rooster's late scratching left twenty-one contestants — nine dogs, three chooks, five cats, two pigs, a pony and Shorn Connery. Half the dogs wore wigs with holes cut out for their ears and all three chooks were trying to shake off bonnets. She began to get excited. Even with Mayor Bullock on the judging panel she was in with a chance — and the mayor was wearing his Chutney Division First Prize rosette, so he might be in a good mood. Tommy Mobsby's pig — done up to resemble the Prime Minister — looked like her stiffest competition. But Tommy had helped her clean up Shorn Connery earlier in the marshalling yard, so it was okay if he won.

Pollo spotted her dad alongside Sherri and Will right behind the line of orange bunting, big grins on their faces. She gave them a wave. Seeing Will made her think of Benson Bragg. She couldn't wait to show Will the photo she'd just snapped of Benson behind the tents.

Principal Piggott took her seat on the judges' platform next to Mr Wise who ran the stock-feed store and Mayor Bullock. The crowd quietened. Deafening marching music suddenly blasted from a speaker and, as owners tried to calm their pets, the volume was hastily lowered. Eventually, Pollo's friend Draino brought her pony under control and the parade began.

The contestants shuffled around the ring to the crackling military music, past the judges, keeping plenty of distance between one another. Beside Pollo, Shorn Connery in his dinner jacket moved with a suaveness that would have made James Bond proud, only stopping to sniff the air when they passed Will, Sherri and Joe di Nozi. When everyone had completed a lap of the ring, the music, mid-crescendo, stopped.

The audience milled as the judges conferred over their clipboards. One or two red-cheeked supporters called out suggestions and their friends laughed cheerily. Draino's pony lifted its tail from under its dragon costume and delivered a load of manure onto the parade ground, drawing hearty applause. Eventually, Principal Piggott stepped up to the microphone.

'A big thank you to all the contestants here today for a marvellous parade — and by contestants, I'm not referring to the human variety!' She waited till a few people chuckled politely. 'The judges have finally managed to reach a decision. Without further ado, I call Mayor Bullock to the podium to present the awards.'

Mayor Bullock levered himself from his chair and swaggered to the podium where three boxes of varying heights were positioned. He ran his gold-ringed fingers over the junction at which his youthfully lush, flaxen toupée met his scalp, checking the wig was sitting straight — a habit he'd not been able to shake. An elderly volunteer with a large metal tray bearing three medals — in bronze, silver and gold — came to stand solemnly beside him.

Principal Piggott cleared her throat. 'In third place, we have Raine Dodd with her pony, Prancer, who is looking splendid today as a medieval dragon.' The crowd clapped heartily as Draino led Prancer to the podium, where Mayor Bullock, his winner's rosette blooming from his lapel, placed the bronze medal over her head and shook her hand.

Pollo bent down and whispered in Shorn Connery's ear. 'One more to go then it's us, old buddy!'

'In second place,' beamed Principal Piggott, 'as James Bond 007, it's the most debonair sheep in the district, Shorn Connery and his owner Apollonia di Nozi!' Pollo's heart sank for an instant, but then she heard Will's *whoop-whoop!* and saw all the smiling faces and couldn't help feeling proud. She led Shorn Connery to the podium and, holding onto his lead, stepped onto the second-highest box, leaving Shorn Connery at ground level in front of her. Mayor Bullock shook her hand — not smiling nearly as broadly as he had for Draino — and Pollo waved her silver medal to the cheers of the onlookers.

A hush fell over the audience, broken only by a raven's *arp-arp-aaah*. 'And in first place —' Principal Piggott paused for dramatic effect, '— a contestant I'm sure everyone agrees looks distinctly like our Prime Minister, we have Hamlet the pig and his owner Thomas Mobsby!' A worthy winner, thought Pollo, clapping enthusiastically along with the happy mob. Tommy climbed onto the highest box and shook hands with Pollo and Draino, a huge grin crinkling his face.

Mayor Bullock lifted Tommy's gold medal from the tray with his ring-bedecked fingers and held it up to the audience, waving it like a magician about to perform a trick. The medal dangled and flashed in the afternoon sun. Suddenly, from out of nowhere, came a *whoosh-whoosh-whoosh* and a whir of black feathers. A raven swooped down at Mayor Bullock's hands, its leathery clawed feet extended. The assistant holding the tray yelped and dropped it with a clang onto Mayor Bullock's foot. Prancer whinnied and jolted, pulling Draino off her box. Shorn Connery, his eyes rolled back, and Hamlet, looking gleeful, belted in opposite directions, either side of Mayor Bullock. They wheeled around him, their leads trailing. The raven — which Pollo now saw was the one from earlier with a wayward feather — hopped about on the ground between them, trying to snatch the dropped shiny medal. Mayor Bullock windmilled his arms at the horde of beasts. The raven flapped its way to Shorn Connery's rump — where his dinner jacket didn't reach — and took a quick pluck of wool.

Shorn Connery shot across the parade ground and through the rope barrier, dragging it and its little orange flags with him. The raven flurried upward, alighting on Mayor Bullock's head, where it crouched, its neck stretched for balance, its talons hooked into the plush carpet of hair beneath. Mayor Bullock stumbled backwards — onto Hamlet who was still sprinting laps around the podium. The pig sent up an ear-splitting squeal. With two beats of its wings, the raven flew off, glided a short way and landed on the fence-post near its mate — the tuft of Shorn Connery's wool in its beak and something floppy dangling from its claws.

Mayor Bullock regained his balance and tapped the microphone. 'Order! Order!' he barked.

People turned to look at him. Gradually the hubbub petered away. Silence. A camera clicked — Pollo's. People began covering their mouths, their eyes bright above their hands. More cameras clicked and whirred. More people began to chuckle.

The mayor plucked a starched handkerchief from his breast pocket and dabbed his face. He opened his mouth to speak but stopped. Slowly his eyeballs rolled up toward his forehead where a breeze was drifting coolly. His eyes widened as his fingers crept to his hairline. He explored his scalp gingerly with his fingertips. Then he began flat-handedly slapping his dome in the search for something lush, soft and shiny — his precious toupée.

Laughter erupted from the mob. The mayor strode to where Principal Piggott stood watching, her hanky over her mouth, her shoulders shaking. He snatched the daisy-covered hat from her head, plonked it on his own and dashed as fast as a stout fellow can to the dark privacy of his big black car. He revved the engine, did a three-point turn and *vroomed* away, bumping across the field, sending up sprays of dirt.

Arp-arp-aaah! The ravens flapped their glossy black wings and disappeared too, heading for the forest.

CHAPTER FOUR

Will and Pollo leaned back against the tombstone in the Riddle Gully cemetery, Pollo flipping through her notes from their day at the fair. Beneath them lay the bones of Elspeth Mary Turner, 'Beloved wife of Henry Thompson Turner', who'd come into the world in 1812 and departed it in 1899. It was their favourite grave. They figured it must contain someone who'd had a happy outlook on life if she'd lasted eighty-seven years back in those days; plus, the lupins nearby were extra lush. Relieved of his dinner suit, Shorn Connery tore at a patch of the purple weeds a little way off.

'You'll have fun with your column in this week's *Coast*,' said Will.

Pollo's eyes lit up. 'Best embarrassing photo of Mayor Bullock ever!' she said. 'I have my faithful assistant

Shorn Connery to thank once again!' She dug out her camera and showed Will the photo she'd taken of the raven and the mayor in a flurry of feathers and fake hair.

Will pointed to the forest across the meadow from the cemetery. 'I'd say that toupée's lining a nest somewhere in there by now,' he laughed.

'And look what else I've got,' said Pollo. 'I didn't have a chance to show you earlier. I took it on my way to the Pet Parade.' She scrolled back to the photograph of Benson on his hands and knees peering beneath the back wall of the white elephant stall. 'You can tell it's Benson Bragg,' she said, 'Who else around here dresses like that?'

'And likes hip-hop music,' added Will, taking the camera and zooming in. 'See this logo on the sleeve? It's the one I was telling you about. Twisted Lips. It's on the front of his T-shirt too. I was face-to-face with it when he pulled me out of the rollercoaster car.' He studied the photo. 'What d'you think he was up to?'

'I have a theory,' said Pollo, lowering her voice, though they were always alone in the cemetery. 'All the stall-owners kept their valuables at the back of their tents, away from everyone passing by out the front. All Benson had to do was poke his head under the back wall, grab what he wanted and be on his way. He was probably crawling along looking for an opportunity when Shorn Connery and I sprang him.'

'He might have found one,' said Will.

'What do you mean?'

'An opportunity,' said Will. 'HB said Mr Crisp who ran the garden stall was missing a wad of money.'

'That's it then! It must have been Benson Bragg.'

'To be fair, it's happened before. His wife's paranoid and hides things without telling him. Three years ago, according to HB, the money turned up in the bottom of a plant pot, and last year they found it months later in a coffee thermos — a bit mouldy but okay. Still ... It could be ...'

'Even Mrs Crisp couldn't be that silly a third time, surely!' said Pollo.

'You wouldn't think so,' said Will.

Baa-aa-aah! Shorn Connery had stopped chewing and was looking towards the forest.

'What's he spotted?' said Will. 'Bats? It's about time they came out of their winter hideaways.' Squinting, he scanned the gloomy twilight sky.

'I can't see any,' said Pollo. 'Can you?' Pollo peered in the direction suggested by Shorn Connery's snout.

Suddenly, against the backdrop of the forest, Pollo discerned a dark thin shape, like a tree-trunk — but one that could walk — moving toward them. She dug an elbow into Will's ribs and whispered. 'Look! It's him — Benson Bragg! He's been hiding his stash in the forest!'

The youth was picking his way through the meadow toward the graveyard. As he walked, his neck jerked, chook-like, and with each step, his left foot gave a quick waggle before it planted on the ground.

They stared at him swinging his arms, bobbing his head, waggling his foot. Will leaned closer to Pollo. 'Is he ... dancing?'

'I do believe he is,' said Pollo, 'in his own special thief-like way.'

*

As Benson drew near, Will and Pollo could see that he barely had his eyes open — just enough to jig his way around the gravestones. And whatever song was playing through his earphones, he was half-singing, half-mouthing the words with passion like he was the band's front man himself.

Shorn Connery remained rooted to his spot among the long grass, a stalk of lupin dangling either side of his snout. Suddenly Benson, no more than three metres in front of him, did a twirl on one sneaker. His hands flew over an invisible drum kit ending in a cymbal clash delivered through his front teeth. *Tss-tsssss!*

Baa-aa-aah!

Benson leapt vertically and yanked out his earphones. Shorn Connery stared at him, unblinking. 'What the ...?' cried Benson. He spotted Will and Pollo sitting on Mrs Turner's tombstone. 'You two! What are *you* doing here?'

'Admiring your moves,' said Pollo, getting to her feet. Will did the same, giggling nervously.

'Punks!' said Benson.

'Unco!' said Pollo.

'Dweebs!' said Benson, a smile creeping onto his face.

'Doofus!' smirked Pollo.

Benson pointed to Pollo's unruly head of springy hair. 'Fuzzball!' he said, grinning and jigging from the knees up.

Will was beginning to feel left out. 'Thief!' he blurted.

Both Pollo and Benson jerked their heads toward Will. *No!* thought Pollo. She hadn't gathered her facts yet! It was way too early for a direct assault! And here they were alone in a graveyard with night closing in, with a kid much bigger than them — were they *whiskers* on Benson's top lip? — who knew she had evidence against him in the camera bulging in her hip pocket. Her hand drifted down to cover it.

Benson tugged his cap tight down onto his skull and glared at Will. 'What'd you call me, Punk?'

'Seef!' Pollo scrambled. 'He called you a seef! He lisps, the poor thing. You've got to feel for him sometimes.'

'Yeth!' said Will desperately. 'I didn't mean to inthult you ... Honethtly!'

'Sounded like thief to me,' Benson grumbled. 'There's not even any such word as "seef".'

'Yeah, but how old are you?' said Pollo.

'Sixteen. What's it to you, Fuzzball?'

'Ah, well,' said Pollo, 'that explains it. See, we're only thirteen —'

'Nearly fourteen!' interrupted Will, flinching as Pollo's elbow found his ribs.

'— thirteen, and in our language a seef is someone who wears their cap sideways ... like you!'

Benson cocked his head to one side. 'Seef,' he repeated. He tugged the bill of his cap lower over his left ear. 'Succinct. Kind of dignified. I don't mind it.' A smile curled onto his face. 'See, if he'd called me a *thief* I would've smashed in Punk's teef!'

He saw Pollo and Will exchange worried glances. 'That was a joke.' He grinned at Will. 'You're the kid who lost his lunch at the rollercoaster today, yeah?'

'*The* kid? The only one?' said Will.

'Yep. Just you. You're distinguished.'

'Great,' sighed Will.

Pollo had plenty of investigating to do. 'So, what's it like working on a rollercoaster?'

Benson grunted. 'S'okay. It wasn't my idea, but. My uncle made me. Said I had to earn my keep.'

'Your uncle,' said Pollo. 'That's Mayor Bullock, right?'

Benson grunted again. 'Small towns,' he muttered.

'And you're staying with him?' asked Pollo, easing into her enquiries.

'Uh-huh.'

Will winked at Pollo conspiratorially. 'How come?' he said. 'Are you being *punished* for something ... I mean, thumb-thing!'

Benson frowned and began cracking his knuckles.

Pollo jumped in. 'He only means that a lot of people in Riddle Gully aren't too keen on your uncle, and it

would be a punishment, sort of, to have to stay with him.'
She glared at Will. 'You don't need to say anything more,
Will. You really *must* rest that sore throat of yours.'

'My thore throat?'

'All that screaming on the rollercoaster, remember?'

'Oh yeah. Thorry.'

Benson leaned over Will, bunching the neck of Will's
T-shirt in his fist. He glared from Will to Pollo and back.
'You, Punk! You, Fuzzball! Do you think you can mess
with me? I'm not stupid!' He let go of Will and shoved
his hands in his pockets. He tilted his head back, looking
to the darkening sky, breathing sharply. Suddenly he
dropped his gaze back to them.

'You know what? I *am* being punished for something.
Whatever you've heard is true. I'm a thief; I'm evil; I
can't be trusted. As soon as my gran turns her back I'm
going to clean her out!' He turned away. 'This place and
its gossip make me want to puke.'

'Oh yeah?' said Pollo, pulling out her notepad. 'It
might be gossip to you, but if someone's going around
stealing from everyone it becomes kind of important to
us.'

'Going around stealing?' Benson scowled. 'Here?
You're making it up.'

'Why else were you listening in earlier when we were talking about Will's stepdad being a police sergeant?'

'Curiosity,' he mumbled. 'Kills cats, not people.'

'Well, why were you crawling around behind the stalls? Yeah, I saw you. It's handy for you, I bet, that we small-town folk are so trusting with our things.'

Benson glared at Pollo and Will, a tinny trace of music leaking from his dangling earphones into the damp twilight air. He opened his mouth as though to say something ... then shut it again. Shorn Connery snuffled at the long grass around Benson's hi-tops but he didn't seem to notice.

Pollo waited, her pencil poised. Benson suddenly jabbed his finger at the notebook. 'You can think whatever you like and you can write whatever you want to write in that ... that lame journal of yours. It won't change who I am.'

He turned to go but discovered that Shorn Connery had developed a taste for the laces of his left sneaker. He waggled his leg but Shorn Connery hung on grimly, enjoying the strange meld of flavours in the dirty shoelace.

Pollo seized the opportunity. 'So you don't deny it then! It is you nicking all the stuff and stashing it in the forest!'

'I'm not denying anything,' said Benson, in a tug-of-war with Shorn Connery. 'And I'm not apologising to anyone in this mangy little town — not to my uncle and especially not to you. You can write that in your pad and stick it up your jumper!' There was a tearing sound as Benson's shoelace ripped free of Shorn Connery's molars. 'Gotta go, Fuzzball, Punk,' he said. 'It's a nice clear night — I've got a lot of stealing to do.' He jammed in his earphones and slouched away.

Shorn Connery stood looking after him. *Baa-aa-aah!*

'Don't bother with him, old buddy,' said Pollo. 'He's bad news.' She tousled the thick wool between Shorn Connery's ears. '*You*, on the other hand, were brilliant once again — stopping him from leaving. I'd never have wangled that confession out of him otherwise!' She turned to Will, her eyes bright. 'You heard him! He practically took my notepad and wrote this week's *Coast* column for me!' She began scribbling in her notepad. 'I'm writing it all down so I don't forget a single word.'

'He's a strange one, alright,' said Will. 'I wonder if we could find where he hides his stash. We could, you know, double-check our suspicions.'

Pollo shrugged. 'No need. He admitted to everything.'

'Well, he didn't deny it,' said Will.

'Same thing,' said Pollo. '*And* he said he wasn't apologising for anything.'

'Not to *you*, especially!' said Will.

'And that I could write what I wanted about him.'

'And stick it up your jumper!' added Will.

'You know, Will,' said Pollo, her eyes narrowing, 'not every single word he said was relevant.'

'It wasn't?'

'No. And I'd just as soon you left it to me to sort out what was and wasn't. I *am* —'

'— Youth Reporter for the district,' said Will. 'Yeah, yeah.'

Pollo slipped Shorn Connery's lead over his head. They began picking their way across the cemetery toward the track that ran behind the houses in their street, shivering as the temperature of the spring evening quickly fell.

'Listen, Will,' said Pollo. 'Do you think you could wheedle a few details out of your stepdad about what exactly has gone missing? But don't tell him why you want it! I want my story to be breaking news — a masterpiece of investigative journalism! Something people will talk about for years!'

'I s'pose I could try.'

'Brilliant!' said Pollo. 'I'll make an assistant super-sleuth of you yet, Will Hopkins!'

CHAPTER FIVE

Pollo had to wait until Thursday to see her story on Benson Bragg in print. As soon as the home-time siren went, she pedalled through town and up the main street to Sherri's shop — the Riddle Gully Second-Hand Emporium Specialising in Maps, Curios and Local History — where she and Sherri routinely looked over Pollo's latest column, hot off the press.

Pollo knew Sherri through her Aunty Giulia. But unlike Aunty Giulia, who was all about manure and stock breeds, Sherri had piled-high brightly dyed crimson hair and dangly earrings that tinkled when she laughed — which was often. Sherri was a bit like a mother to Pollo, the way she talked about stuff and looked out for her. Pollo was sure her mum would have loved Sherri too if she'd still been around.

Pollo grabbed a clean copy of the *Coast* newspaper from the metal stand on the footpath and flung open the glass door of the shop, setting the door's bell jingling and Bublé the budgerigar twittering.

'Goodness!' cried Sherri from behind her desk. 'It's Wonder Woman come to rescue me from a terrible fate!'

'Sorry! Didn't mean to scare you! It's just that this week's column is the juiciest I've come up with for quite a while,' said Pollo. She found her column and spread the newspaper in front of Sherri, then came around to look over the older woman's shoulder as Sherri read aloud.

DIAMOND JACK'S BACK

Riddle Gully has been rocked of late by a string of jewellery thefts. Has the infamous bushranger Diamond Jack, ancestor of Mayor Bullock and his family, risen from his grave to help himself, once again, to the riches of Riddle Gully, as he did over a century ago? Items gone missing over a two-week period include earrings, wristwatches and an antique emerald ring.

Fortunately, this reporter, in a rollercoaster investigation, tracked down the culprit — who cannot be named for legal reasons — and obtained a full confession to the thefts. In addition, he was heard by this reporter to say: 'It's a nice clear night — I've got a lot of stealing to do.' He also expressed his intention to rob an elderly relative. The culprit, who has a recent history of stealing, showed no sign of remorse. Police have been informed and the matter is now in their hands.

Pollo jabbed the page. 'See how I got "rollercoaster" in there, Sherri? Hint, hint, eh?'

'And the mention of Mayor Bullock's family and the elderly relative,' murmured Sherri. She looked up at Pollo. 'Is this article about who I think it is? A certain young man who's staying with his grandmother?'

Pollo grinned and nodded. 'You got it! I never mention Benson by name because he's only sixteen. But read on! It's when you read *both* articles that you see how cunning I've been.'

In other news, a raven provided last Sunday's Riddle Gully fair with a novel climax. As Mayor Bullock presented the gold medal to local farming boy, Thomas Mobsby, the bird swept down and relieved the mayor of his infamous toupée. (See photo and full results of fair on page 7.)

The bird eluded capture and is thought to be nesting comfortably in the vicinity of Riddle Gully. Fortunately for the mayor, his 16-year-old nephew, Benson Bragg, has been staying in Riddle Gully for approximately two weeks. In a suspension of usual school routines, he appears to have been hunting for his uncle's missing toupée, Mr Bragg having been spotted in the forest on the outskirts of town.

'See how the times match up,' said Pollo, 'and the bit about his suspension? I slipped that one past the editor, I did!'

Sherri blew through pursed lips. She rose from the

desk and opened the door to Bublé's cage, inviting the little bird onto her finger. 'Mayor Bullock's not going to like this one little bit,' said Sherri, scratching Bublé's head, 'or dear old Mrs Bullock, for that matter. You've as good as told anyone who can put two and two together about Benson's suspension from school and the reason behind it — that bit about his recent history of stealing. And you've pointed the finger at him for these Riddle Gully thefts. Do you think that was wise?'

'But that's the thing,' said Pollo. 'I haven't just used what you told me. I've done some real investigating — like Woodward and Bernstein!'

'You know about the Watergate scandal? That happened in the seventies. I barely remember the details myself.'

'Woodward and Bernstein were Mum's heroes, according to Dad. They brought down a crooked USA president, after all.'

'Well, if you've done some proper investigative reporting like your mum would have, good on you, I suppose.' She stroked Bublé's back with her thumb. Pollo saw the frown flickering on Sherri's face.

'What's wrong? Don't you like the stories?'

'It's not that. It's just that there's ... there's something a bit fishy about Benson's confession. Are you sure he meant it? He wasn't just being ironic, was he?'

'I-what?'

'Ironic. You know, when you say the opposite of what you mean in order to show you mean the opposite.'

'What?' squawked Pollo. She goggled at Sherri. 'Why on earth would anyone talk like that?'

'I agree, it gets messy sometimes,' said Sherri. 'I went on a date once with a fellow a friend had described as "charmingly modest" when she actually meant he was a tiresome toad who boasted about himself all evening. I didn't pick up her tone over the phone. Golly, I couldn't wait for dinner to finish. I even skipped dessert.' Sherri held Bublé up to eye level. 'We haven't made that mistake again, have we Bublé?'

'But you yourself told me Benson was a thief. That he'd stolen something at school.'

'Yes,' said Sherri. 'That's partly what worries me. Poor Mrs Bullock. I hope she speaks to me again. She loves that boy to bits.'

'Huh! Even when he's planning to rob her too?'

'To be perfectly frank, Pollo, I simply can't accept that part of your story.'

'The truth is sometimes hard to accept,' said Pollo.

'True, but I wonder ... would you have suspected Benson in the first place if I hadn't shared that snippet from his grandmother; if I'd kept my mouth shut?'

Pollo folded her arms in a hunch. 'Well, a reporter has to start digging somewhere.'

'Hmmm ... Heaven forbid that the truth be allowed to sit quietly and mind its own business.' Sherri carefully returned Bublé to his cage.

Pollo narrowed her eyes. 'Are you being ironic, Sherri?'

Sherri sighed. 'Yes, Pollo. I'm afraid I am.'

*

Pollo pedalled away from Sherri's shop, her face twisted in a frown. What did Sherri know? Of course a reporter had to sniff around, dig stuff up — otherwise no one would know anything about anything. And, of course, she'd have suspected Benson sooner or later. She'd practically caught him red-handed behind the tents, hadn't she? His confession was just the icing on the cake. Pollo wheeled around a corner and found herself pushing towards the edge of town. What she needed was a long, hard pedal up the hill to the lookout. It usually helped her let off steam.

When she reached the turn-off to the lookout, she

saw something that sank her spirits even further. It was a familiar sight outside the roadhouse. In front of the bowsers, a sheep truck idled. The back of the truck was loaded with animals four tiers deep, the twitching ears and sniffing snouts of those on the top tier just visible. Down the side of the truck, legs protruded between the slats. The sheep were jammed together so tightly that, had the truck suddenly turned a somersault, it was doubtful the poor creatures would have budged. Lucky Shorn Connery wasn't there to see it.

Just then the roadhouse door opened and two figures emerged — one in shorts, navy singlet and work boots and, following him, another in a baseball cap, black T-shirt, hi-top sneakers and ...

Hang on! Pollo squinted. That was no truckie! Benson Bragg ambled across the forecourt, bobbing his head to whatever was pumping through his earphones. He swung up into the cab alongside the driver and swivelled his cap's bill to the front to shield his eyes. The driver revved the truck's huge engine, eased onto the hardtop and rumbled away, the doomed sheep staring dolefully behind.

Good riddance, Benson Bragg, thought Pollo. Riddle Gully's better off without you.

CHAPTER SIX

Pollo and her dad, Joe, stood by the car at the end of their driveway in the pink glow of early evening. Pollo was twitchy with excitement. Friday night at last. She'd been waiting ages for this moment. Joe di Nozi shuffled and scratched. He'd been dreading it. He cleared his throat.

'If you're asked to do something that makes you feel uncomfortable, just leave, okay? Walk away. You get what I'm saying?'

'Uh-huh. Walk away.'

'Because if a person doesn't respect your limits it means they don't respect you.'

'Limits. Respect. Roger.'

'Who's Roger?' Pollo frowned at her father.

'Roger? It's two-way radio talk for "I understand".' Joe di Nozi rubbed his nose. 'Where do you get all this stuff from anyway, Pollo?'

'Sherri.'

'Sherri. Of course, I should have guessed.' In the car's side mirror, Joe adjusted the collar poking from his jumper and checked his nostrils.

'Well, she knows a lot more about dating than you do, Dad.'

'No need to rub it in. I have my pride.' He put an arm around his daughter's shoulders. 'Don't fret about me, love. I'll have a good time and I'll see you at lunchtime on Sunday. It's me who has to worry about you.'

'Dad, I have my books, a stack of DVDs and a fridge full of junk food. Not to mention a science assignment. And Aunty Giulia and Uncle Pete or Sherri are only a phone call away if I need them. We've been through all this.'

Joe di Nozi sighed. 'I hope I'm doing the right thing. Two nights away ...'

'You've been wanting to meet Wanda face-to-face for ages, Dad, and she lives too far away to do it any other way. You can't drive hundreds of kilometres to Wanda's place and then across to her cousin's wedding in one day. You'd be asleep by nine o'clock with your head in a plate of pavlova.'

'Sometimes I wonder what you got me into with this online dating,' said Joe. 'I don't know if I'm up to it.'

'Dad, don't be dumb! As Sherri was saying, if you can tramp through paddocks rescuing animals all day, you can manage a simple date with a lady.'

'Sherri? You've been talking to her about it?'

'Of course! Sherri says you just need to build up your confidence. Apparently, you have an inner tiger that needs unleashing.'

'An inner tiger?' Joe picked a dog-hair off his jumper.

'So she says. In fact, Sherri helped me pick out Wanda.'

'Oh, no! You two were going through my dating site?' gasped Joe.

'Sure!' said Pollo. 'You don't expect me to sign you up to a service and not monitor things, do you? That would be irresponsible. I don't want you having your heart stomped on by some Jezebel. We had to delete quite a few responses. Sherri said Wanda was perfect because she wasn't so gorgeous-looking that you'd go all gaga and lose the plot.'

'But Sherri ... she's ... I've wanted ... it's plain embarrassing, Pollo!'

'There! That's it precisely! If you're ever to ask

Sherri out on a proper date, Dad, you have to get in some practice. Asking her to help you deliver that foal last week doesn't count.'

Joe stared mournfully at his shoes.

'You'd better get going,' said Pollo. 'Wanda will think you've chickened out.'

'Chickened out ... yes. Listen, sweetheart,' said Joe, edging away from the car, 'I'm really not keen on abandoning you like this. It's a long time to leave you to your own devices.'

Pollo opened the car door, picked up her father's travel bag from the driveway and threw it in. 'Don't you dare make *me* an excuse for not getting on with your life!' She pushed him firmly down into the driver's seat and closed the door. 'Wanda — Wedding — Fun. Remember?'

Her father wore an expression Pollo usually saw when an animal needed to be put down. 'Fun ... hmm ... yes. Okay then ... well ... goodbye, I suppose. Love you.' With a sigh, he turned on the ignition.

Pollo leaned in and kissed her father's cheek. 'I'll have a quiet weekend reading and doing homework and watching movies and scoffing all the things you never let me. And I won't answer the phone, so there's no point calling to see how I am! Bye, Dad! See you Sunday.'

Joe backed slowly down the driveway and onto the street. Pollo waved patiently as he idled there a bit longer before chugging up the road towards the setting sun. Only as he turned the corner did the smile drift from Pollo's face and her thumbnail find its way to her teeth.

A loud *baa-aa-aah* drifted over the roof. Poor old Shorn Connery! It was way past time for his daily walk to the cemetery. She hurried inside. It was just as well they were going out somewhere. Seeing her father drive away to spend the weekend with a lady made her feel a bit odd — even if she had put him up to it.

CHAPTER SEVEN

Shorn Connery practically broke down the back gate getting onto the path leading to the cemetery. They half-walked, half-ran in the fading light, the back fences of houses on one side of them, lightly wooded bushland on the other. When Pollo saw Will's running shoes poking from behind Mrs Turner's gravestone she slipped the rope from Shorn Connery's neck and watched him gallop across the lumpy field, sending clouds of midgies swirling. He headbutted Will, knocking his sketchpad off his lap, then began snuffling and chomping at a patch of nearby lupins.

Will was brushing dirt off his sketchpad when Pollo caught up. 'I thought you might have been and gone,' he said. 'How come you're so late?'

'Dad wasn't in a hurry to get going on his big date. I

practically had to push his car up the street. I hope she's as nice as she seemed on the dating website.'

'Who? This Wanda lady?'

'Yeah.'

'Nice, but not too nice, eh?' said Will. 'Not stepmum-forever type of nice.'

'You've got it,' said Pollo. 'Oh, I don't know what I want. Poor Dad.'

'Don't sweat about it now. It's only a first date.'

'Hmm ...' said Pollo. 'What brings you here, anyway? I thought you'd be busy packing for your weekend with your dad. It'll be the first time just by yourselves since your little brother came along, won't it?'

'My *half*-brother, the rug rat. Yeah. He's kind of hard to ignore. It'll be good.' Will twirled a pencil between his fingers. 'I was hoping to make a start before I left on some wildlife sketches I have to do for art school. Trouble is, the only wildlife I can see is that ugly raven over there. Look, it's even got a dodgy feather.'

'Hey!' said Pollo happily. 'That bird's my hero! It's the one that stole Mayor Bullock's toupée!' She called over to it. 'Thanks, cobber! I owe you!'

'Well, it's got a dead rabbit now,' said Will. 'It's grossing me out.' Shorn Connery, too, seemed unimpressed, watching the bird from the corner of his eye.

Pollo moved a few steps closer to the raven. It had its feet planted on the corpse of something that, a few days before, had been romping in the graveyard. It was now tearing at the remains with its beak. It stopped foraging and cocked its head to assess Pollo with a flat white eye. She backed off.

'When are the sketches due?' she asked, settling down beside Will.

'They're meant to be in tomorrow. Luckily I'm skipping art school tomorrow though. If I go into Maloola first I don't get into Canberra till late, and Clive says it's a long drive to the camping spot.' Will grinned. 'Works out doubly well, actually. I don't want to run into Benson Bragg in Maloola again! Not this weekend! After your column yesterday he won't be feeling very sociable.'

'Don't worry,' said Pollo. 'I saw him hitching a ride on a sheep truck yesterday. Looks like he's leaving town.'

'Good thing you wrote what you did,' said Will. 'You scared him off. Good job!'

'Hang on a minute,' said Pollo. 'You said "again".'

'Did I?' said Will. 'When?'

'You said you didn't want to run into Benson in

Maloola *again*. When did you see him there before?'

'Oh that,' said Will. 'It'd been bugging me ever since we saw him at the rollercoaster, and this morning it came to me. Two Saturdays ago, I went to Game Zone after art school. He was playing a wicked game of Monster Mash right next to me. You should see him play Monster Mash, Pollo. He's like a magician!'

'*After* art school?' said Pollo. 'You sure it wasn't before art school, or during a break, maybe?'

'Course not,' said Will. 'It's just there's often a bit of time to kill before the twelve-thirty train back to Riddle Gully.'

'Oh dear,' said Pollo. 'That's not good. Not good at all.'

'What's wrong?' said Will. 'What'd I do this time?'

'Nothing. But that's when Aunty Giulia's ring went missing — right on lunchtime.'

Will doodled on his sketchpad. 'So what you're saying is, it couldn't have been Benson who stole your grandmother's ring ... because Benson was standing next to me in Game Zone at the time.'

Pollo nodded. She suddenly blurted, 'You never said you'd seen Benson in Maloola!'

'I didn't work it out till today. Besides, you never

said when the ring disappeared!'

'Maybe,' muttered Pollo. 'I guess we still have the other thefts to pin on him.'

'And his confession,' said Will.

'Mmm ... that confession,' said Pollo, rubbing her chin.

They sat in silence, idly watching the raven jumping about the carcass, clamping it with its clawed feet, jabbing it with its beak. *Arp-arp-aaah*. The bird began hopping backwards, away from Pollo and Will. As it did, the slanting sun's rays caught something shiny being dragged in the grass.

'What's it got?' said Pollo.

'Looks like a collar ... but rabbits don't wear collars.'

Pollo got to her feet and stepped slowly toward the raven. It hopped away, the object in its beak tinkling, its white eyes fixed on Pollo.

'That's no rabbit,' said Pollo, standing over the raven's abandoned carrion. 'That's Terrence Schultz.'

'Who?' said Will, scrambling to his feet.

'Terrence Schultz — Mrs Schultz's cat. Mrs Schultz came into Dad's surgery the other day asking if anyone had brought him in. He must have died out here in the cemetery.'

'Well it's the right place to cark it, I guess,' said Will. 'D'you think Mrs Schultz might like to have his collar?'

'Good idea! She loved him like crazy,' said Pollo. But as the two of them edged forward, the raven jumped back, as before, Terrence's dangling bell glinting beneath its beak.

'Don't look at it,' said Pollo. 'They say wild animals don't like eye contact.'

They edged forward, their faces averted, sneaking sidelong glimpses of the bird. But with each of their steps, the raven hopped further away, the collar clamped in its strong black beak.

From the forest fifty metres away came the mournful *arp-arp-aaah* of another raven.

'That's probably its mate,' said Pollo.

'Telling this one here to quit messing about and bring home dinner,' said Will.

Will and Pollo half-crouched, motionless, watching the raven. It hopped in a wide arc back to where Terrence rested in pieces. It laid the collar in the grass nearby and resumed pecking at the rotting flesh, a whisper of wind rustling the soft, oily-black hackle-feathers at its throat.

'Now!' they both yelled.

They rushed headlong. The raven tilted its head,

regarding them with an icy eye. As they closed the gap, Will dived at Terrence's collar like a baseballer sliding for home. There was a flurry of flapping wings and the bird flew beyond reach. As Will spat and wiped dirt from his tongue, it circled above them, the bell in its beak, the sun flashing off it like a beacon.

They craned their necks, tracking the raven's flight from the cemetery to a large red gum near the entrance to the Diamond Jack hiking trail at the edge of the forest. The raven flapped onto a high branch and hopped sideways toward a thick clump, hard to make out in the failing light, but almost certainly a nest.

'Wow! That bird was one cool customer!' said Will. 'It wasn't going to lose that bell for quids. I wonder if they've ever trained ravens to nick stuff. I've seen 'em do it with monkeys in the movies. Ravens would be good at it — as long as whatever they were after was shiny.'

'And no one would suspect them,' said Pollo quietly. She stepped around Terrence to Mrs Turner's tombstone. She slumped down on the mossy granite and began nibbling at her thumbnail.

'It's like they're undercover!' said Will, sliding down beside her. 'No one thinks of a mean-looking old bird like a raven wanting pretty things.'

'No,' said Pollo. 'Not you, not your stepdad, no one in Riddle Gully and, worst of all, not me.'

'Why so glum?' said Will. 'It's only a cat's collar. It wasn't going to bring old Terrence back to life or anything.'

Pollo looked at him. 'What's the bet, Will Hopkins, that if we were to climb that tree over there we'd find everything that's gone missing in the past few weeks, including my grandmother's ring.'

Will exhaled in a long whistle. 'So you don't think Benson ...'

Pollo shook her head.

Off in the distance, the ravens cawed in the last light. *Arp-arp-aaah.*

Will pointed to the distant red gum. 'And that ravens' nest ...'

Pollo nodded.

'It would make sense,' said Will. 'The randomness of what's been reported — single earrings and stuff. There's probably a lot more junk that's been taken but people only missed the valuables.'

Pollo chewed her bottom lip. 'I wrote that story so that everyone who knew Benson would think he was the culprit. I as good as told the world he'd been suspended from school and why. And now he's run away from Riddle Gully in disgrace.'

*

They hurried back across the graveyard, through the long grass damp with evening dew, dragging an irritable Shorn Connery who'd had his eye on several more lush lupins. At Will's place, his mum Angela and his stepfather Sergeant Harry Butt, a.k.a. HB, were sitting at the kitchen table, each with a small glass of beer in front of them. Angela was chopping vegetables while HB went through the mail.

'Hey Angela, HB! Listen to this!' panted Will. Pollo and Will babbled out the story of Benson hitching a ride out of town, and the raven at the cemetery, and Will standing next to Benson at Maloola, playing Monster Mash, when Pollo's Aunty Giulia's ring went missing.

'Game Zone!' said Angela. 'So that's where all your pocket money's been going! Since when have you started going there, Will?'

'Were you listening at all?'

'Maybe to the wrong bits,' said Angela, nibbling a slice of parsnip.

Will rolled his eyes at his mother.

'Hell's bells,' said HB. 'Only the other day Pollo told

me I should bring Benson in for questioning. Good thing I bided my time, eh?' HB scratched his head. 'You really believe the loot's up a tree? It's worth looking into, I suppose. First thing Monday, I'll get hold of a fire truck with a long ladder.'

'Monday?' said Pollo. 'But it's only Friday night! Meanwhile, Benson goes the whole weekend with everyone thinking he's a criminal!'

Pollo caught Angela and HB swapping glances. Angela bent her head to a vigorous bout of carrot chopping. They may as well have been shouting through megaphones — *Thanks to you!*

'It's not good, I agree,' said HB. 'But another day or two won't make much difference. For all his problems at school, the lad seems to have his head screwed on right.'

'But what about him hitching a ride on a sheep truck? He could be anywhere!'

HB pinched his earlobe between thumb and forefinger and stroked it thoughtfully. 'He's sixteen, lass. He's allowed to go places. He might have even gone back home.'

Angela beheaded a celery stick. 'What about that raven with the poky-out feather, HB? You should bring the bird in for questioning!'

Will shook his head. 'We're serious, Mum!'

'Sorry!' said Angela. 'The thought of HB taking mug shots of a raven just makes me giggle!' She imitated HB's deep voice. 'Sir, Ma'am, whatever you are. Please stop squawking and turn side on to the camera.'

HB took a sip of beer and put his glass down carefully. He spread his big hands on the table. 'Look kids, these are the facts as I see them. This ravens' nest will still be there on Monday. My deputy's gone bush for a few days. And I can't get the volunteer fire service out on a whim — not on the weekend. They'd have my guts for garters.'

'A whim? This is an emergency!' cried Pollo. 'Benson was in trouble before. My dumb story might push him over the edge — even if he is back home with his mum. We need to prove to everyone he's innocent!'

'Now, now,' said HB. 'Remember we may not even find anything up in that nest.'

'Just a dead cat's collar,' said Angela.

'Yes ... err ... that's right.' HB rose to his feet and rested a hand gently on Pollo's shoulder. 'Ease up a bit, eh, lass? These things have a way of sorting themselves out.'

Pollo stomped along the track to her back gate, lighting the way with her pocket torch. *Ease up a bit?*

That was grown-up talk for sit on your hands and do zip. And, as far as she knew, no one ever changed anything doing that.

CHAPTER EIGHT

Pollo's breath was still misting her bedroom window when Shorn Connery's bleating roused her from a dream in which a tiny Benson Bragg — cap, hi-top sneakers and all — was being carried aloft in the gnarly claws of a raven.

A single thought clanged in her head as she opened her eyes. *Poor Benson!* She frowned at the ceiling, wishing Will wasn't going away this weekend so she could talk over things with him more. Angela and HB might be right. There might be nothing in the ravens' nest but Terrence Schultz's grubby old cat collar ... but she might be right too.

She reached for the notepad in which she'd recorded Benson's words at the cemetery. After ten seconds of reading she threw it on the floor. Will was spot on.

Benson hadn't confessed to their accusations at all. He simply hadn't denied them. And he sure hadn't known what he said would end up in a newspaper.

Pollo threw on her clothes and beanie and went into the kitchen to make some toast. On the Vegemite jar was a sticky-note from her dad — *Love you! Have a good day!* She chewed slowly, staring blankly at her science assignment spread on the table from the night before. It just wasn't right! Here she was tucked up in her nice safe home, knowing people loved her, while Benson was out there — who knew where? — copping the blame for things he hadn't done.

She shoved the rest of her toast in her mouth and gathered her things, her cheeks bulging. She headed for the back door where Shorn Connery greeted her, butting her knees.

'We might have to wait till Monday to prove the real thief was a raven, old buddy,' said Pollo, slipping his rope lead over his ears, 'but we don't have to wait till then to start clearing his name! Come on, we're going to pay someone a visit!'

She strode down the road towards town, Shorn Connery trotting eagerly ahead. Things might sort themselves out the way HB suspected — but they'd do it faster with a little boot from her.

*

'How dare you tie that farm animal to a lamppost, blocking a public byway, and then waltz up to my front door to quiz me about my personal matters!' Mayor Bullock stood on his top step, his temporary toupée perched crookedly on his head, a lump of boiled egg-white shivering on the collar of his woollen dressing gown.

From the hallway the reedy voice of Mrs Bullock drifted beneath his armpit, followed by her snowy-white head. 'Now Orville, dear. Try to be civil. It's not often we have young folk come to the door.'

'Something I've strived hard to achieve, Mother. And no —', with his hip Mayor Bullock blocked his mother from joining him on the step, '— Miss di Nozi would *not* like a cup of tea.'

Pollo swallowed. 'Please, can you just tell me if Benson's okay? Do you know where he is? The thing is, I'm almost certain now that Benson —'

'It would seem, Mother,' interrupted Mayor Bullock, 'that Miss di Nozi, after bandying our family's dirty laundry to the district, has now come to enquire after Benson's whereabouts and wellbeing.'

'That's very sweet of you dear,' said Mrs Bullock, pushing her snowy head through the gap between her son's armpit and the doorjamb.

'No, Mother! It is not sweet. It's impertinent!' spluttered the mayor. He glared at Pollo. 'Benson went home and is in his mother's care, such as it is. That is all I shall say on the matter.'

'He went home?' said Pollo. 'Really?'

'That is what I believe I indicated,' said the mayor.

'We got an electric letter,' said Mrs Bullock. 'It was on the line. That's right, isn't it Orville?' She swivelled her head up to look at her son.

'It's called an *email*, Mother!' huffed the mayor. He turned to Pollo and pursed his lips. 'My sister emailed me on Thursday evening informing me she'd been discharged from hospital earlier than expected and my nephew had caught the train home. I trust that settles the matter.'

That was no train Pollo had seen Benson climbing into. 'The train?' she repeated.

'Do you intend echoing every word I utter?' snapped the mayor. 'Yes. The train. A machine that runs on rails. A convenient conveyance for the masses.'

'Orville was in a lather about it,' said Mrs Bullock.

'And Benny went off without his little telephone. I'm sure Orville would have let him have it back if he'd known Benny was leaving.'

The mayor grunted. 'If the rapscallion had stayed here I'd have knocked some self-discipline into him. Going about his pilfering ways right under my nose ... compromising my reputation and my authority in Riddle Gully!'

'But that's the thing!' blurted Pollo. 'I don't think Benson *did* any pilfering! Not here in Riddle Gully. There's a pair of ravens building a nest in the forest and —'

'But you said he had, yourself, dear,' said Mrs Bullock gently. 'You wrote it in the newspaper — more or less.'

'Well I wish I hadn't,' said Pollo. 'The raven did it! The one with a sticky-out feather!'

'Keh-heh-heh!' Mayor Bullock's laugh rasped like a shoe scuffing on pavement. 'You're back-pedalling now, eh? "The raven did it" indeed! That's what I call a desperate measure.'

Pollo pulled herself up as tall as she could. 'It's what I call having the courage to admit I was wrong.'

'The youth of today!' scoffed Mayor Bullock. 'No backbone! Too soft. And no stomach for good, hard discipline when it's needed!'

'Orville! Where are your manners? You were young once too, as I recall, and —'

'I was never any such thing!' snorted the mayor, 'And I would appreciate it, Mother, if you didn't interrupt me only to criticise me!' He turned to glare at Pollo. 'My wayward nephew is, alas, beyond my control and no bizarre ornithological fantasy story will change that. Whatever misfortune befalls him from now on, he'll have only himself and his lily-livered mother to blame. Now, if you don't mind, I'm going back to my breakfast. I suggest you, Miss di Nozi, go home and play with your dollies.'

Mayor Bullock hustled his mother away and shut the door firmly in Pollo's face. Pollo stood on the step, the doorbell a millimetre from the tip of her nose. *Play with her dollies?* How about her *chainsaw*? She turned and stomped down the footpath where she began untying Shorn Connery, muttering furiously.

'Caught the train home, did he?' She plucked at Shorn Connery's rope. 'So why was he hitching a ride on a sheep truck then — a sheep truck headed in the wrong direction? Tell me that, eh!'

Baa-aa-aah!

'Exactly!' fumed Pollo. 'The mayor has cornflakes for brains and clearing Benson's name is going to be even harder than we thought. Benson's on the loose out there, probably thinking the world's against him. And that kind of thinking brings trouble and big, deep holes. We have to find Benson, old buddy, before he gets into real strife.'

Pollo freed Shorn Connery from the lamppost and began marching toward the train station. She'd check the timetables and work out a plan — one she'd have to execute alone. Of all the weekends for Will to go to visit his dad, why did he have to pick this one?

CHAPTER NINE

Benson Bragg poked his head from the run-down caretaker's shed behind the Royal Arms hotel. It didn't sound like there was anyone around but you had to be careful. He stretched and rubbed where the concrete floor had made him numb. Hugging himself against the damp ocean wind that never seemed to stop, he walked across the yard to the tap, dodging old bits of machinery and broken bottles. The sick-sweet smell from the abattoir drifted down to him, even from three kilometres away. Or was it the dumpster at the pub's back door? He unscrewed the hose and, between slurps, rubbed water on his face and neck. It was stinging-cold but it helped clear the grit of the night. He replaced the hose as he'd found it, covering his tracks. The shed was as good a place to stay as he could hope for right now and he didn't want to blow it.

He patted his pocket out of habit, and wished he had his phone so he could check in with Kal. But his uncle had locked it away somewhere when he saw Benson texting during one of his lectures. He probably had about twenty unread messages from Kal by now, wondering what was going on. Benson felt weird without a phone. Kind of naked. Hey! Like in the dream he just remembered! He was at school wearing only his boxers, and they'd kept getting smaller and smaller. What was *that* about?

His second morning in Princeville and already he, too, hated the place. It seemed like everyone he talked to was on their way somewhere else or was stuck here and bitter about it. The guys at the abattoir entertained themselves in petty, nasty ways — especially the ones who'd been there a while. He hadn't seen a smile since he'd arrived — not that he'd lit up the place himself.

But he'd keep his head down and stick it out because payday wasn't till Tuesday and he'd left himself short of options. In one way, he'd be better off hitching back to the city the same way he'd hitched here from Riddle Gully. On the other hand, what was the rush? He might be a fish out of water here in Princeville — but at home, just like in Riddle Gully, people called him a thief.

He wiped his wet face with his T-shirt and checked the time on his iPod. Grabbing a tin of baked beans from the shed, he plugged in his earphones and set off up the road.

CHAPTER TEN

Will was on the platform, his blue backpack leaning against his leg, when Pollo arrived at the station. Beside him, his mother Angela jigged restlessly in the brisk breeze, her hands in her coat pockets. Not wanting any adults to start asking questions, Pollo tied Shorn Connery to a fence amid long grass a little way down from the platform and hurried under the station arch into the waiting room. She stood on tiptoes next to a window, from where she could hear Angela giving Will last bits of advice.

'When you get off at Two Wells, don't muck around, love,' she was saying. 'Get yourself over to the other platform right away. The train to Canberra waits for no one. And don't even think about stopping in at the café, even if it does have the best raspberry muffins in the universe.'

Will licked his lips with a faraway look as Angela continued. 'You picked up those carrot sticks and sandwiches from the kitchen bench, I hope.'

'Um ... I might have overlooked the carrots.'

'Oh, Will! You've got your phone, though? And your emergency money is somewhere safe?'

'All in my backpack,' said Will. 'Don't worry, Mum. Nothing's going to happen.'

At that moment Angela's mobile rang and Pollo took her chance. She poked her head around the corner of the waiting room. 'Pssst!'

Will looked around. Pollo flapped her hand, beckoning Will. 'Benson's run away!' whispered Pollo. 'I got it from Mayor Bullock himself just now!'

'Mayor Bullock told you that?' said Will.

'Well, not exactly,' said Pollo. 'But he told me his sister, Benson's mum, had emailed him to say Benson had caught the train home on Thursday.'

'But you saw him getting on a sheep truck!' said Will.

'Exactly! A sheep truck on the road to Maloola, not the city,' said Pollo.

Will scratched his chin. 'Do you reckon the mayor was telling the truth? You don't think he was trying to trick you?'

'I didn't get that impression. He didn't seem to care where Benson was, as long as he wasn't under his roof.' Pollo gnawed a thumbnail. 'It's more likely Benson faked the email.'

'Faked it? But he'd have to have been at his mum's computer for that, wouldn't he?'

'Sometimes I wonder about you, Will,' said Pollo. 'Anyone can send an email from any computer pretending to be someone else if they know the person's password. And adults usually have really easy ones they won't forget — like their birthdays and stuff.'

Will nodded sagely and made a mental note to change his own. Just then, the train hissed into the station, the first three carriages for passengers followed by twenty or so goods vans with big sliding side-walls, some open, some shut. Pollo and Will heard Angela calling him.

'I'd better scoot,' said Will. 'If I miss this train Angela will kill me. The rest of the day's services are out so she'd have to drive me to Two Wells!'

'Out?' squeaked Pollo. 'When you say "out", do you mean cancelled? All the way to Maloola?'

'Yeah, for track maintenance.' Will pointed to the wall. Above the timetables was taped a sign in black texta. The next train wasn't until Monday morning.

'Well, like I say — gotta go! See ya next week I guess,' he chirped.

Pollo scrunched her face. 'I can't wait till Monday!' She raced from the building, leaving Will alone in the waiting room scratching his head.

Two minutes later, the platform guard blew the all-aboard whistle. A minute after that, the train began to edge slowly from Riddle Gully station. Ten seconds after that, Pollo, dodging Shorn Connery's kicking hind legs, heaved her faithful assistant's rear end into an empty goods van and scrambled after him, sprawling on her stomach on the grubby floor as the train picked up speed.

CHAPTER ELEVEN

Baa-aa-aah!

Shorn Connery, tied to a railing in the goods van, didn't like Pollo's latest case one little bit. He scuffled back and forth on his stick legs with the rocking of the train, his yellow eyes rolled back in their sockets. Pollo huddled near him, her woollen beanie pulled low, watching the fields, trees and fence-posts strobe past. Her cheeks were mottled mauve and her teeth clacked as the morning chill whipped through her.

As the train rattled on, Shorn Connery settled enough for Pollo to lean into the thick wool around his neck. She wished he'd lie down so she could snuggle into him like a hot-water bottle. Had she gone too far this time? She hadn't planned and she wasn't prepared. She had no firm idea of where to find Benson, and her only tools were her notepad, pencil and pen-knife — what she'd stepped out of the house with when she'd gone to visit Mayor Bullock. No phone, no money, no information! It was just her and her panicky sheep, freezing to death, hurtling across the countryside to who knew where.

Well, actually, that was one thing in her favour. She did know where — to Two Wells and on to Maloola. That was the good thing about trains. They didn't wander off. She blew warm air into her cupped hands and tried not to think of Will in his carriage up ahead somewhere, toasty warm and, by now, almost certainly tucking into his sandwiches. And she tried not to think of Benson — except to hope that somehow Mayor Bullock was right, that he really had gone back to the city.

Pollo unravelled her beanie so it covered her whole face. She hugged her knees and tried to imagine she was holding a mug of steaming cocoa. The train clattered onward, slowing down as it passed through tiny towns, but speeding up again without stopping.

Eventually, Pollo sensed the train slowing more than usual. She rolled up her beanie to see the stockyards of Two Wells coming into view — mobs of stony-coloured sheep penned behind steel-rail fences topped with barbed wire. As the train approached, they scampered to the farthest corner of the pen, kicking up dust; as the carriages rolled by, they stared unblinkingly, as one. From the open door, Shorn Connery stared back at them silently.

A whistle sounded and they eased into Two Wells station. Pollo thought about getting off to have a quick look for Benson but, remembering there were no more trains to Maloola till Monday, decided against it. The trucks that ran the highway past Riddle Gully seldom detoured into Two Wells anyway. Benson was far more likely to be in Maloola.

Wary of being seen, Pollo crawled on her hands and knees to the van door and peeked out, relishing the sun's faint warmth. It was silly to hope to spot Benson, but you never knew. On the station platform by the head of the train, people were already walking briskly in different directions. Will would be among them, finding the right platform for his train to Canberra.

In the grey dirt of the stockyard alongside Pollo and Shorn Connery's van, a lone ewe, dusty-white but for a black left ear, stood apart from the mob of sheep. The tip of her snout was lifted toward them. It swayed delicately side to side, catching the strange new scents that had rolled to a stop in front of her.

Pollo sat back on her heels and smiled at the sheep. 'Hello there, Ear!'

Meh-eh-eh! The black ear twitched.

Baa-aa-ah! Shorn Connery, roped to the end wall of the van, began tugging at his short lead. 'Sorry old buddy, I forgot about you,' said Pollo, getting up to lengthen his rope. 'I guess you want to stretch your legs while you can.'

As soon as Pollo loosened his lead, Shorn Connery broke free and clattered to the open van door. He stood rigid, sniffing towards Ear. Ear stared, transfixed, from the stockyard up at Shorn Connery. Shorn Connery half-closed his eyelids so that the vertical slots of his pupils were barely visible. His wet, hairy nostrils quivered.

Just as Pollo caught the end of his rope and wrapped it round her fist, Shorn Connery flung himself forward, landing with skittering hooves on the narrow stretch of loose gravel between train track and stockyard. To avoid being yanked out onto her face, Pollo had no choice but to jump down with him. Dragging his mistress over the loose stones, Shorn Connery barrelled forward, snorting, his ears pricked forward, to where Ear waited, her hooves stamping. The two animals stood nose to nose either side of the barbed-wire-topped barrier.

Meh-eh-eh! Ear blinked her stiff white lashes and twitched her black ear.

Shorn Connery flicked his handsome long tail. *Baa-aa-ah!*

At that moment, a sharp whistle-blow cut through the air, signalling the train's departure. Pollo leaned back on Shorn Connery's rope lead. 'C'mon, boy!' she huffed. 'We have to get back aboard. There's no time for these shenanigans!'

Meh-eh-eh!

Baa-aa-ah!

'Forget about her, old buddy,' pleaded Pollo. 'She's from the wrong side of the tracks. It'll never work out!'

Meh-eh-eh! Ear spun both ears and glared icily at Pollo.

Baa-aa-ah! Shorn Connery ground his hooves into the gravel.

Pollo's guts clenched. They couldn't stay where they were! The train was kilometres long and the gap between it and the fence wasn't much wider than she was. She looked at the snarly barbed wire. There was no climbing over — not in a hurry. It was either get back on the train or pin themselves hard against the fence as the train whooshed past, millimetres from their noses. And Shorn Connery's stuck out further than hers. She grabbed her faithful assistant around his middle and pulled, trying to keep calm, trying not to picture the swish and hiss of steel wheels flying by.

Suddenly Pollo heard the thudding of running feet. She craned her neck to see, from the other side of the goods van, a blue backpack fly through the opening and skid across the floor. Behind it appeared a grinning face.

'Will!' she cried. 'What ...? But ...? What are you doing here?'

'Can I give you a hand?'

'Can you ever!' Pollo passed Shorn Connery's rope up to her friend. 'Of all the times to fall in love, Shorn Connery picks now! He won't budge. Quick, you pull and I'll push!'

A second whistle trilled — longer than the first. With Pollo shoving from the ground and Will tugging from above, they wrangled Shorn Connery, bawling and writhing, back aboard. Will lashed him to the rail.

Suddenly, the train hissed and jerked forward. Pollo flung herself upward, clawing the van floor with her fingertips. As the ground began to roll away beneath them, she hung suspended over the lip of the opening, her legs thrashing in midair. Gradually the train jolted into a smoother rhythm. Will gripped Pollo's arms, wedged his feet against the edge of the big sliding door and leaned back. They were just passing the 'Thank You for Visiting Two Wells' sign when Pollo, kicking and huffing, rejoined the early Saturday service to Maloola.

Meh-eh-eh!

Baa-aa-ah!

Meh-eh-eh-eh-eh!

Baa-aa-aa-ah-ah!

The train trundled onward, Shorn Connery bleating forlornly as the stockyard — and Ear — dissolved from view.

CHAPTER TWELVE

'Why aren't you going to Canberra!' shouted Pollo as the train accelerated. 'Angela and HB will murder you! Clive will murder you! Someone will murder you, anyway!'

Will smiled and shook his head. 'No they won't.'

'Why not? It's months since you saw your dad.'

'Clive rang just as we left Riddle Gully,' said Will above the clanking of the train. 'He says he's got the flu so camping's off. Tiff came on and said it was only a man-cold and I should come anyway, but if my dad doesn't want me around ...' Will's voice trailed off.

'Some people feel sickness more than others,' Pollo offered, rubbing her goosebumpy arms. 'They can't help it.'

'Yeah. He's one of them — a wuss.' Will unzipped his backpack and drew out a fleecy jacket. He plonked it on Pollo's lap. 'Here, take this. I'm warm enough in my windcheater.'

Pollo pulled on Will's jacket eagerly. 'Thanks!' She prodded Will's sagging backpack with a foot. 'Do you even have a change of clothes in there?'

'Nup. I was going on a father-and-son camping trip, remember? The stinkier the better. Plus, I needed room for my art stuff.'

'Always the artist,' said Pollo.

Will smiled wryly. 'Always the artist with overdue art assignments.'

'How did you even know we were on the train?' said Pollo, pulling her beanie down to her eyebrows.

'Huh! You ran off at Riddle Gully like you had a lizard in your daks, so I guessed something was up. Then when I got off at Two Wells I heard Shorn Connery. It all came clear what you were up to — and it was totally clear that I wasn't going to call Angela and mizzle back to Riddle Gully just 'cos my dad's a wimp. I figured the more people looking for Benson, the better.'

'When will you tell your mum and HB you haven't gone to Canberra?'

'Hmm ...' Will drummed his chin with his fingers. 'I might forget to mention that for a while.'

Pollo tucked her knees to her chest and grinned. 'That's what I like to hear!'

*

The train rattled onward, crops and sheep paddocks swishing by. 'So, what's your plan?' said Will.

Pollo peeked through the slit between beanie and jacket. 'I was hoping you wouldn't ask. I'm ashamed to say, I haven't got one.'

'But when you jumped on the train at Riddle Gully it was to find Benson and tell him we knew he was in the clear, right?'

'And to say sorry for ever printing that stuff about him.' Pollo picked at a thumbnail. 'I still don't understand why he told us he'd done the robberies,' she said. 'That was crazy. I'd never have written my story if he hadn't said that stuff.'

Will pulled a sandwich from his backpack. He picked out the tomato and tossed it to Shorn Connery, who swallowed it in one sniff. 'Maybe not so crazy,' he said. 'More kind of sad.' He bit and chewed. 'Look at it from his side. Maybe he's already feeling like a scumbag for stealing whatever it was he stole at school. Then we come along and he thinks, "I'm already a scumbag — what difference does it make if I'm a bit bigger one?" You know, like when you start on a packet of biscuits and eat more than you mean to — and then you think, "Well, I'm already a pig — I may as well finish the packet."'

'You do that, too?' said Pollo.

'Plus, he gets to stir us up at the same time,' said Will. He took another bite, and added through his mouthful, 'Course, he didn't know it would end up in the newspaper.' He held out the squashed sandwich remains to Pollo. 'Want some?'

'Err, no thanks.' Pollo folded her arms. 'I still don't get why it's Benson who gets to feel sorry for himself.'

'Haven't you ever done something you wished you hadn't?' said Will.

'I get cranky with Dad sometimes,' mumbled Pollo.

'Well, what if, instead of coming back into your real un-cranky self afterwards, something happened and you got stuck being cranky?' Will leaned towards Pollo, his eyes spooky-wide. 'It's like a nightmare. You know the sort of person you really are but no one else seems to. Soon everybody's treating you like you're a crank, even though you know deep down you're not.' Will popped the last of the sandwich into his mouth. 'You'd be pretty keen to get your old self back, wouldn't you?'

'I'd definitely want my old self back.' She pulled out

her notepad and pencil. 'So your theory is that Benson got this idea of himself as a thief —'

'A scumbag.'

'— a scumbag ... and then, between his uncle and us, he couldn't get his old self back? He got stuck feeling like a scumbag?'

Will shrugged. 'I reckon that could be it.'

Pollo shook her head. 'I'd just tell my uncle or whoever to go count the holes in a crumpet.'

'Not everyone's as ... as ... sure of themselves as you,' said Will.

Pollo eyed him sideways from beneath her beanie. After a moment she huffed, 'You might have shared all this wisdom of yours earlier.'

Will gazed at the scenery skimming past. 'Didn't know I had it until now.'

CHAPTER THIRTEEN

Benson, in a long rubber apron and rubber boots, leaned against the cyclone wire fence that cut off the abattoir from the surrounding farm. The spring sun was warm on his shoulders and the song pulsing through his iPod brought happy memories of rehearsing in Kal's garage with the band. But the stink of the slaughterhouse nearby stuck like glue in his nostrils no matter what track was playing.

A little way off, the workers who liked a smoke with their mug of morning tea — which, as far as he could tell, was everyone but him — huddled in a grey haze, swapping jibes and laughs, the women in a clump to one side of the courtyard, the men in a clump on the other.

He was hungry but no one was handing out scones and jam, that's for sure. At Gran's place, he'd never eaten so much excellent food in his whole life — one good thing about staying there; the only thing other than Gran herself. When his mum landed in hospital just as his suspension was about to kick off, and with his dad away up north, everyone thought it would be such a great idea for him to go and stay in Riddle Gully. Everyone but him. It had turned into a nightmare. Uncle Orville collected him and lectured him all the way to Riddle Gully, shutting up only for that half hour he'd had business at Maloola. But it got way worse once they were at Gran's place. Whenever Gran gave Benson a hug or told him a story about when he was little, his uncle got angry, or made out she was old and stupid and had her facts wrong. He acted like he was jealous ... like he was worried Gran mightn't have enough love to go round.

Benson didn't care what his uncle thought of him. But when he talked to Gran like that ... man, it made him want to give him one. But all Benson could do was sit there and say nothing, 'cos if he did say anything to defend Gran, it just made his uncle carry on worse. He felt like a total mongrel either way.

Nah, he just raked up trouble at Gran's. Even without that girl writing her story in the newspaper he couldn't have stayed. He didn't want to run out on Gran like he had, but he was better out of the way.

'Hey kid! You ignoring me?' Benson became aware, over the music in his ears, of a gruff voice. He turned to see the Duke, as the other workers called him — a stocky man in his forties. The Duke was a few metres away and holding out a packet of cigarettes, a teasing look in his eyes under his wiry raised brows.

Benson pulled out an earphone and shook his head — 'No thanks'. He resumed staring at the sky. The joke was old already — they knew he didn't smoke — but the other men bent their heads together and chuckled gleefully every time.

'Into your second day and ya haven't come said g'day. Bit posh for us are ya?'

This was off-script, thought Benson. 'No, course not.' He forced a smile at the Duke.

'Then come and have a chat with the boys and me.'

'Sure,' said Benson. He pushed off the fence. The Duke headed for the cluster of workers and Benson followed.

'Only one rule,' said the Duke as the men shuffled to make room for them.

'What's that?'

'You gotta have a little puff every once in a while to come stand with us.'

There was a round of hard, flat laughs and a few coughs.

Benson shook his head and stretched a smile. 'Nah, no way. It killed my granddad. Sorry.'

The Duke took a drag and allowed the smoke to drift slowly from the corner of his mouth. 'We got a problem then. If you stand over there all by yourself, how do we know what sort of a fella you are? How do we know we can trust you? The boys here get toey if a bloke don't join in.' He looked around the grinning group. 'Don't ya, boys?'

The men nodded and smirked.

'But we like to think we're reasonable,' said the Duke. He scratched the stubble of his whiskers slowly, keeping his eye on Benson, thinking. 'How's about ...' — the men looked at one another expectantly and giggled — '... a bit of a prank? Harmless. No one hurt.'

Benson scuffed the ground beneath his rubber boot. 'What kind of prank?'

'All we want you to do,' said the Duke, 'is come back here tonight and take the boss's family portrait from his desk.'

'Here — at the abattoir? But I'd have to break in, wouldn't I? I'm not breaking any laws for you,' said Benson.

The Duke laughed. 'You've been breakin' laws sleepin' in the shed out the back of the Royal Arms the past two nights,' he said. 'Yeah, that's right. Tony's missus is a cleaner there. You've been spotted, kid. Lucky no one's put the law onto you already! A door jimmied open here, a lock smashed there — it's all the same to a copper.'

Benson shoved his hands in his pockets and stared at the ground.

'Frankly, young fella,' said the Duke, 'you're a bit on the nose. You wanna warm shower and a nice soft bed, am I right?'

Before Benson could stop himself, he nodded.

'Well, take the photo from the boss's office tonight and Tony's missus will square it so's you get a free room at the pub for a few days — no questions asked.'

Benson imagined the dirt and stink of the abattoir swirling down a plughole. 'Sounds fair,' he mumbled.

'It's more than fair.' The Duke turned to his workmates. 'It's downright charitable of us, wouldn't you say lads?'

The men nodded, smirking.

'Thanks,' said Benson flatly.

'Don't mention it,' said the Duke. 'And then, like I say, we'll know we can trust you. You'll be one of us.'

A siren sounded and the workers began stubbing their butts on the gravel and drifting toward the abattoir door. 'One little thing,' said the Duke.

Benson paused. 'What's that?'

'On your way out, if you happen to see any cash that looks like it needs a good home, it'd help if you were to relocate it with us. It might stop tongues slipping if the boss asks questions. Know what I mean?'

Benson jammed his earphones back in. 'Yeah,' he said. 'I do.'

CHAPTER FOURTEEN

The moment the train hissed to a halt at Maloola, Pollo jumped down. Will shoved Shorn Connery's rear end and they soon had him on solid ground, sniffing the salty air of the seaside town. They scurried along the narrow gap between train and fence until they were close to the platform. As soon as the coast was clear, they scrambled their way up and fell into step with the other passengers. They would have blended right in if they hadn't been accompanied by a sheep.

As they wove through the crowd in the station building, Will kept his eyes on the chequered linoleum floor and dropped back several paces. With a bit of luck, if someone from art school were to spot him, they might not connect him to the girl trying to control the excited ram. Will felt the blood pulsing in his temples at the very thought of it. He'd be as red as a chilli pepper by now. Knowing this, he blushed even more.

'Will! Will Hopkins!' Pollo's voice squawked through the air. 'Why are you all the way back there? Come up here and help me, quick!'

He cranked up his line of sight to see Pollo slithering on the concourse — a newspaper kiosk to one side of her and a flower stall to the other. She was leaning back on Shorn Connery's rope as the sheep, his hooves doing wheelies on the smooth floor, drove full-tilt for the stall, eager to wrap his hairy lips around its juicy spring display.

People edged past sideways, giving them dirty looks. As Will looked on, aghast, Pollo's feet slid from under her. Slowly but surely, Shorn Connery was dragging her — on her backside and gripping his lead — toward the fragrant bouquets in their bright buckets.

Baa-aa-ah! The few people in the station not already staring at them turned around.

'You! Get that animal out of here!' The stationmaster was striding toward them. 'Go on! Skedaddle!'

Will sprang forward and tugged on the rope with Pollo. They stemmed Shorn Connery's charge with his snout millimetres away from a bunch of daffodils. They hauled him to the exit, his hooves leaving four deep gouges in the linoleum, and hurried away from the station.

At the war memorial overlooking the grey ocean near the edge of town, they found a bench where the grass grew long around the nearby trees. Shorn Connery set about mowing it, while Will and Pollo flopped down, looking out at the white-tops being whipped up by the stiff breeze.

'Do you think anyone saw you?' asked Pollo.

'Pollo, everyone in the whole station saw me!' cried Will.

'I mean, anyone who knows you weren't meant to be coming into Maloola today, dummy — like a teacher from your art school.'

'I don't think so,' muttered Will.

'That's good. I wouldn't have wanted there to be a scene.'

Will shook his head. Pollo's idea of a scene clearly differed from his.

'So ... to Benson?' he said.

'And his old self,' said Pollo.

'Where the heck do we start looking?'

'Where would you go if you were him?'

'Definitely the bakery first,' said Will. 'And then

Game Zone, maybe.' He frowned. 'But what if he's just gone on home?'

'If he wanted to go home, as his uncle claims, he wouldn't have hitched a ride down this way,' said Pollo. 'He would have caught a train to Two Wells and changed trains up to the city. All the big trucks take the route that bypasses Two Wells. It's possible, I guess, he jumped off the sheep truck along the highway somewhere and hitched a different ride into Two Wells. But it's more likely he came straight here, I think.'

Will rubbed his stomach. 'Well, I know I wouldn't mind going to the bakery.'

'That's our first stop then. We can ask around.'

'We can't bring Shorn Connery with us though!' blurted Will. 'He'll ... you know ... draw attention. And if Benson sees us coming he won't hang around to have a chat.'

'Good point,' said Pollo. She huddled into her jacket, thinking. 'Hey, I know! Mr Mallard! He's a retired sheep farmer from Riddle Gully who lives close by. One of Dad's old customers. We might be able to leave Shorn Connery with him.'

*

As Pollo, Will and Shorn Connery walked up the

106

footpath, Mr Mallard tipped back his hat and leaned on his spade. 'Pollo di Nozi!' he called. 'That's a fine young specimen of a ram you've got there, girl. Reminds me of one I had in the nineties. Won Best Fleece in Show four years running.'

'This here's Shorn Connery!' beamed Pollo. 'Oh, and this is Will. We've got a bit of business to do in Maloola, Mr Mallard. We were hoping we could leave Shorn Connery with you for a while.'

The old farmer nodded. 'Sure thing! You kids leave the young fella with me and come back for him when you're ready. I'll be going off to bowls later but you kids go on round the back. Side gate's never locked.'

A little later, Will and Pollo emerged from Maloola bakery with a lamington each and no further clue as to where Benson might be hiding. They walked up the main street, eating and keeping a lookout for Benson, asking at any place he might have visited and where a shopkeeper might remember him. No one knew anything nor seemed too fussed at being unable to help.

'I guess he might have changed his mind and made his way home some other way,' said Pollo, looking at the brochures and timetables in a travel agent's window.

'No, I reckon you were right before,' said Will. He

looked up and down the street. 'I've got a hunch he's around here somewhere. He's probably down in the dumps, remember. It figures he'd want to get lost from everyone for a while.'

'If you say so,' said Pollo.

They trudged on until they came to the big glass doors of Game Zone. They stepped inside the cave-like room that flickered with flashing lights. Although nearly empty, it was raucous with sirens, bells and whooping sound effects from the gaming machines.

'What was Benson's favourite machine again?' yelled Pollo above the racket.

'Monster Mash!' said Will.

'Where is it?'

'Through there, behind that wall.'

They wove between the machines keeping as close to the walls as they could, and peeked around the corner. Monster Mash's lights pulsed, but no one was there to appreciate them.

Pollo sighed. 'Come on,' she said. 'Let's get out of here.'

'No, wait!' said Will. He fished in his pocket for some coins.

'Will! We don't have time for that now!'

Will ignored Pollo and walked trance-like across to the machine.

'We've got to keep going!' shouted Pollo.

Will fed a two-dollar coin into the slot, shrugging off Pollo who tugged on his arm. The big panel of lights shimmered into action.

'I can't believe this!' Pollo turned to go. 'I'm going to keep looking for Benson. I'm not standing here while you —'

'Pollo! Look!' cried Will, pointing to the screen. 'Highest score! Bragger Bee!'

Pollo looked. 'What are you on about?'

'Bragger Bee. Bee-for-Benson Bragg! That's got to be him. And according to this, he posted twelve-thousand-seven-hundred-and-ninety-two on this machine the day before yesterday. Wow! My best's only five-thousand-and-forty. I told you the guy's a magician!'

'Let me see that!' Pollo bumped Will aside and stood before the Monster Mash machine, her eyes glowing. 'That's Thursday — the day he left Riddle Gully! So he *did* come here!' She clapped Will on the shoulder. 'Will, my friend, you are a genius!'

'So we're on the right track,' said Will blushing. 'We keep searching.'

'You bet!' said Pollo. 'Bragger Bee — come out, come out wherever you are!'

CHAPTER FIFTEEN

But Bragger Bee didn't come out. Pollo and Will trawled the streets of Maloola asking and looking, but Benson was either hiding or had left town. Eventually they returned to the bench at the war memorial. The breeze off the water had picked up. They huddled shoulder to shoulder, staring out to sea.

'What do we do now?' said Will. 'I guess it's time to go back to Riddle Gully.'

'Shsh!' said Pollo. 'I'm thinking.'

'Well I'm hungry,' said Will. 'I'm going to that roadhouse up there. You want anything?'

Pollo gave a tiny nod, frowning and chewing on her bottom lip.

Will jogged up to the roadhouse on the edge of town. He crossed the forecourt, dodging the patches of oil and grit beside the bowsers. The front window was plastered with advertisements and messages. He bought two meat pies and a Chiko Roll from the pallid-skinned girl behind the counter. He was shouldering his way out when a help-wanted note caught his eye. It was fly-spotted, yellowed and curling at the edges.

```
Princeville Abattoir.
Immediate start.
No experience necessary.
Monday—Saturday. Apply at office.
```

He turned back inside. The girl was now sliding cellophane-wrapped pies into the pie-warmer. He checked her name badge and cleared his throat.

'Excuse me ... err ... Ebony.'

Ebony tucked her hair behind her ears, looked toward the door into the back room and smiled hesitantly. 'Yes?'

'That help-wanted sign for the abattoir over there,' said Will. 'It looks a bit old. D'you know if it's still current?'

Ebony nodded. 'Uh-huh. It's not a nice place to work. People leave there all the time. The sign just stays up.' She looked Will up and down. 'You're not planning to ask for a job there, are you?'

'Me? No ... no way. Just wondering,' said Will.

'Funny. You're the second one's asked about that sign in two days. A guy came in late Thursday and bought two pies, same as you. Then he asked for a pen to write down the name of the place.'

'Was he wearing his cap to one side, d'you remember?' said Will. 'You know, hip-hop style?'

'Yeah. And a black T-shirt with some band logo on the front — a weird painting of a face all the wrong way round,' said Ebony. 'And he kinda danced when he walked. Didn't seem the type for an abattoir job. But I s'pose people got to earn a livin'. And it's not like most of us don't like a bit of lamb when it's cooked up and served on a plate.'

At that moment, a beefy woman wearing a greasy apron came through the fly-strips from the back of the shop. She shot Will a dirty look.

'That's me mum. Gotta get back to work,' said Ebony.

'Thanks heaps, Ebony,' said Will. You've got a great memory!'

'Aw, I dunno about that. Hey, drop by again sometime, eh? Anytime. I'll be here.'

Will jogged back to Pollo, handed her a pie and

told her, between hot mouthfuls, about the sign in the window and what Ebony had told him.

'Will Hopkins, you amaze me sometimes,' said Pollo. 'I couldn't have done better myself! Right then, let's go!'

'Go where?'

'To Princeville, of course. To the abattoir.'

'What? Now? Like, right this minute?'

'Benson will be short of money, so chances are he took a job there. The abattoir operates on Saturdays, according to the job ad, so we might be able to catch him at work if we hurry. It's only thirty or so kilometres up the coast. We can catch the bus.' Pollo jumped to her feet.

Will stayed sitting on the bench, Ebony's words pulsing in his head. *It's not a nice place to work.* 'What about Shorn Connery?' he said, trying to buy some time.

'He'll have to come too. The bus will be nearly empty at this time of day. The driver won't mind. Probably.'

'But maybe we could just come back tomorrow with HB and Angela.'

Pollo looked at her friend wearily. 'You know what adults are like, Will. Benson's not doing anything illegal, remember — not yet anyway. And if you started talking to them about old selves and new selves they'd pat you on the head and tell you to get an early night. Then you'd be stuck in Riddle Gully for the rest of the weekend.' Pollo began pacing up and down. 'We can't risk it, Will. Not with Benson at the abattoir. We need to go now — as a team.'

'A team that includes a sheep,' said Will sulkily.

'Shorn Connery contributes in strange and mysterious ways, Will,' said Pollo brightly. 'Without him falling in love with Ear at Two Wells, we wouldn't be here right now. Think of that.'

Will did ... and found his mind drifting to the Chinese takeaway they often had at home on Saturday nights.

'Shouldn't we, you know, get provisions or something?' He was scraping for excuses now. He wasn't even sure what provisions were exactly.

'If Benson's at the abattoir and we find him soon enough, everything will be simple. We'll be home in time for tea. Come on, let's go get Shorn Connery! Stop talking and start walking!'

Will sighed, heaved himself to his feet and swung his backpack onto his shoulders.

*

They were still two hundred metres from Mr Mallard's house when the bleating of Shorn Connery carried to them on the wind.

'Crikey!' said Will. 'He's mad about something! I hope the neighbours haven't complained already.'

They hurried up the street and knocked on Mr Mallard's door. From the backyard, Shorn Connery bellowed more loudly than ever. 'He's not home,' said Pollo. 'Let's go around the side.'

As they rounded the side of the house, they saw a salt-white sheep in the farthest corner of the yard, backed up against the timber fence. It was closely shorn, as naked as a sheep could get. Pollo gasped.

'That's not ... is it?' said Will.

Baa-aa-aah! The animal suddenly galloped across the lawn at them. It took Pollo out at the knees and stood over her, thrusting its snout at her face and neck, as she lay spreadeagled on the ground. Will began to giggle uncontrollably.

'He's sheared Shorn Connery!' laughed Will. 'Mr Mallard's sheared him! He's only half the size!'

Baa-aa-aaa-aaah!

'Get out of it, old buddy!' cried Pollo, ducking her head side-to-side.

Baa-aa-aaa-aaah!

Pollo rolled on the ground, cackling, trying to dodge her faithful assistant as he nibbled her nose and jabbed his fuzzy snout in her ears. Eventually — with no help at all from Will — she was able to get to her feet and put her arms around Shorn Connery's skinny neck. Shorn Connery huffed short, indignant puffs of air through his nostrils.

'Poor Shorn Connery,' said Pollo. 'He's never been shorn by a stranger before. Mr Mallard's done a good job though. Thorough. I wonder what he did with the wool.'

'There's something over there next to Shorn Connery's lead,' said Will, pointing to the back step of the house.

On a bulging hessian bag was a note. Pollo unpinned it and read: *Dear Pollo, hope you don't mind. Needed to know if I still had the knack. Take the fleece if you want, and give my best to your dad. Sincerely, Harry Mallard.*

Pollo lifted the bag. It was about the size of a pillow, tightly packed with Shorn Connery's wool then sewn closed across one end with bailing string. 'It's not too heavy,' she said, hefting it onto her shoulder. 'Aunty Giulia would want to spin it, I'm sure.'

'Here, give it to me,' said Will, taking off his backpack. 'I've only got a few paints and brushes in here now.'

'Are you sure?' said Pollo.

'It's no problem,' said Will. 'The laugh was worth it. Now let's get on that bus to Princeville before I change my mind.'

CHAPTER SIXTEEN

Pollo, Will and Shorn Connery thanked the driver and clattered from the bus down onto the main street of Princeville. It was after four and the sun was beginning to lose its kick. Litter eddied on the cracked footpaths, whipped by the wind off the sea. The newly denuded Shorn Connery trembled slightly, whether from the cold or the tinny animal smell of the abattoir a few kilometres out of town, Pollo couldn't tell.

They looked around. The bus stop was in front of the thrift shop, its display window filled with outfits their grandmothers might have worn, the lower halves faded from sitting behind glass so long. On opposite corners of the nearby intersection were two pubs, the balcony of one — the Royal Arms — bowed and flaking. Behind it, a church spire streaked with gull droppings rose hopefully. Across the road, overlooking the steely ocean, was a playground, but from the look of the weeds rising around the cubbyhouse and the glass slivers glinting on the old rubber paths, no one had used it in a long time. A swing on hinges in need of oil creaked rhythmically in the damp wind. It looked like a ghost-child was riding it.

Will pulled the sleeves of his windcheater down over his fists. 'Let's go find Benson,' he said. 'I don't want to hang around here any longer than I have to.'

They set off toward the abattoir, the trees either side of the road out of town bending with each swirl of sea air. After half an hour of walking, they came to the gateway of an access road. Above it was a large sign — *Princeville Abattoir*. Nearby, a tree had fallen and pushed down the fence.

'Which way?' Will couldn't help lowering his voice, though no one was around. 'Through the gap in the fence or up the driveway?'

'We've nothing to hide,' said Pollo, not sounding so sure. 'I say we take the driveway.'

'So we're just going to stroll into the office and ask to see Benson? That's it?' said Will.

'Why not?' said Pollo. 'We can say we've got

important information for him.'

They headed up the access road lined with twisted, whispering eucalypts. Above their footfalls they could hear sheep bleating in the distance. Buildings, a gravel car park and an unloading dock, a semitrailer parked alongside, eventually came into view. They forced themselves onward. Shorn Connery shuffled close to Pollo, his hooves barely missing her heels, his ears flattened, his nose waving as the smell of animal fear wafted over them. As they neared the abattoir, beyond the truck and adjacent to the main building, they could see two large holding pens. The one nearer the truck was empty. From the pen further away, a thousand-odd eyes stared at them bleakly.

They edged around the car park toward the main entrance, their every move tracked by the bleating, scuffling sheep. Running between the holding pens and what looked to be a slaughterhouse was a concrete platform. It was separated from the pens by a high steel fence that curved inward at the top, back toward the animals, preventing any escape.

A tangle of small trees and shrubs formed a garden of sorts leading to the entrance steps. Pollo scratched Shorn Connery between the ears. 'This is where we tie you up, old buddy.' She and Will picked their way through the bushes and had just tethered Shorn Connery to a tree at the back when a loud siren wailed. Instinctively, they dropped to a crouch.

'Home time,' whispered Will, when the noise had faded. 'Are we too late?'

'This works out even better,' said Pollo. 'We can grab hold of Benson out here and follow him till we make him see sense!'

The big front doors were flung open. Men and women began filing out and heading for their vehicles, joking and jostling with one another, checking their phones or just hurrying, head down. After several minutes, a figure in a baseball cap and hi-top sneakers plodded down the steps, plugged in earphones, shrugged into himself and began trudging toward the long driveway — and them.

Pollo rammed her elbow into Will. 'Here he comes!' She shifted, ready to spring from the cover of the garden.

But Will grabbed her jacket, yanking her back. 'Wait!' he hissed. 'Someone called out to him. That guy over there, see?'

A heavy-set older man was sauntering across the car park to Benson, his face in a haze of tobacco smoke. Benson, only metres from Will and Pollo, stopped and waited, grinding at the gravel with the heel of his sneaker.

'About tonight, kid.' The man tapped the side of his nose as he approached. 'Just a heads-up. The fellas are a sociable lot, but if you were to front up tomorrow morning empty-handed, I can't guarantee things mightn't get a little ... let's just say ... awkward for you.' He clapped a hand around Benson's shoulders and pointed to a red ute. 'Jump in with me, eh? We can run over things on the way back to town.'

The man steered Benson away. Together they climbed into the ute. The engine kicked and gurgled. Pollo and Will watched as the older man twisted his head to reverse. Benson, though, stared down at his lap. Slowly they motored down the driveway and out of sight.

Will lowered the branch of a shrub with a forefinger to eyeball Pollo. 'What was that about, do you reckon?'

'I don't know,' murmured Pollo, 'but it looks to me like Benson's old self is in strife.'

They were still crouching in the garden when a fellow, who from his clean shirt and trousers looked to be the boss, locked the front doors, crunched across the car park to his vehicle and drove away.

Will stood and stretched. 'At least we know for sure Benson's working here,' he said. 'And you heard that geezer — we know he's coming back in the morning.'

'Unless we can get to him first,' said Pollo.

Just then, a dog woofed. Once. They couldn't see it, but it sounded big. Shorn Connery's ears flattened sideways.

'Drats!' hissed Pollo. 'I didn't think of a guard dog.'

'Let's get out of here,' said Will. 'I think it must be on the inside. But all the same, we don't want to get it started!'

'I'm with you there!'

Pollo and Will untied Shorn Connery and cautiously stepped from the garden. Shorn Connery, though, remained rooted to the spot, his snout waving in the air. From the holding pen in the distance came the single sad cry of a sheep. *Meh-eh-eh!*

Shorn Connery's ears pricked forward. *Baa-aa-aah!*
Meh-eh-eh-eh!
Baa-aa-aa-aah!

'Look!' said Pollo, pointing. 'It's Ear!'

'Here?' cried Will. 'The guard dog? Where?' He darted to a tree and began scrambling up, bark showering down around him.

'No! Ear!' said Pollo. 'The ewe with a black ear that Shorn Connery fell in love with at Two Wells.'

Meh-eh-eh-eh!

Baa-aa-aa-aah!

Will hugged a low branch. 'And that's why he's —'

'— refusing to move ... yes.'

'Just great!' said Will, returning to earth with a thud. 'Do you think he knows why she's here? That tomorrow she'll be ... you know ... L-A-M-B C-H-O-P-S.'

Pollo put Will's letters together in her head and shuddered. 'He might have the general idea. This place doesn't smell like a farm. If you ask me, it smells like death. The sheep out here would sense something bad's going to happen to them.'

Meh-eh-eh-eh! Ear had pushed her way to the front of the mob, her head now pressed against the bars of the fence adjacent to the empty expanse of the first holding pen. Pollo and Will could see her ears — one white, one black — twirling. She stared their way hopefully.

Baa-aa-aa-aah! Shorn Connery lunged for the fence.

'Pollo,' said Will, looking at the sun slanting over the paddocks, 'we have a much better chance of finding Benson while it's still light. And there's that guard dog. It might have friends on the outside.'

Just then, they heard another woof — like a second warning shot.

Pollo turned to Shorn Connery, wrapping his rope lead around her fist. 'Sorry, old buddy. We have to go.'

Together, Pollo and Will shunted Shorn Connery away from the fence and up the driveway to the main road, Shorn Connery bleating all the way.

CHAPTER SEVENTEEN

Will and Pollo tramped into Princeville, Shorn Connery in tow. Dark clouds were piling on the horizon. As they'd done at Maloola, they crisscrossed its few side streets, keeping their eyes peeled for Benson and the red ute in which he'd left the abattoir. They hunched into their collars against the wind that drove in from the sea, snaggling their hair, burning the tips of their noses.

'My Pop would call this a lazy wind,' said Will. 'It doesn't bother going around — it just goes straight through you.' Pollo laughed, cupping her hands and huffing into them.

But they had no more luck in Princeville than Maloola. The light was fading and the mini-mart was about to close. They went inside and bought bread, cheese and a packet of Ginger Nuts, keeping as much of

Will's emergency money back as they could bear. When they stepped outside, the sun had all but signed off for the day. Fine needles of rain began pricking their cheeks.

'Let's head back to that playground,' said Pollo. 'It had a cubby.'

They reached the lonely playground and hunkered down in the derelict cubbyhouse. It was a little warmer there, especially with Shorn Connery blocking the doorway, looking hopefully back in the direction of the abattoir.

'I guess there's only so much we can do,' said Will, staring hungrily at the cheese Pollo was digging at with her pen-knife. 'Is this where we ring our parents?'

Pollo stared at him in astonishment.

'Dad will be at the wedding by now! I'm not going to wreck his big date after all the trouble Sherri and I took to get him on it.'

'HB and Angela wouldn't mind coming to get us,' said Will.

'And bringing us back in the morning so we can find Benson at the abattoir?' said Pollo. She arched an eyebrow at Will. 'And that's after you've explained to them why you're in Princeville and not Canberra!'

'Oh, yeah,' said Will. 'I forgot about that.' He wrapped

some bread around a piece of cheese and took a bite. 'I know! We catch the bus back to Maloola and ask Mr Mallard to put us up!'

'You haven't learned much in the year you've been living in the country, have you Will?' said Pollo. 'There's no bus back to Maloola until tomorrow morning.'

'What?' yelped Will. 'You never said!'

'You never asked,' said Pollo.

'So we're stuck here in this dump of a place?'

'If you were being a miserable pessimist, you might say that,' said Pollo. 'On the other hand, an optimist might say we've enhanced our opportunities of finding Benson. We could do another sweep of Princeville later. We might still find him.'

Will snorted and shoved the rest of his bread and cheese into his mouth. He pulled his phone from his backpack and began scrolling through phone numbers with his thumb, his cheeks bulging. Shorn Connery, standing at the door, bleated mournfully into the wind.

'Take another example,' continued Pollo cheerily. 'If you were a miserable pessimist, you might say there was no point going back to the abattoir tonight to rescue Ear because we'd never pull it off. On the other hand, an optimist might say —'

Will spun his head to look at Pollo. 'What? There's no way, Pollo! You can't be serious! I'm calling Angela right now!' With a flourish, he pressed the call button on his phone. He held the phone to his ear, glaring defiantly at Pollo. Outside, beyond the cubby walls, the ocean growled and the empty swing creaked.

Pollo cut more cheese while Will waited for his mum to pick up. After a minute, he put it down and mumbled, 'She's got it switched off.'

'That's because she thinks you're safe in Canberra,' said Pollo. 'What's the bet she and HB are planning a lovey-dovey night in your absence? You don't want to go near that, do you?'

Will hastily shoved the phone into his backpack like it had suddenly sprouted fangs.

'So what do you want to do?' said Pollo. 'Sit here all night and freeze to death, or come back with me to the abattoir and spring Ear?'

'There's other stuff I can do,' said Will sullenly. He tapped his backpack. 'I've brought my paints, remember. I'll finish one of my art assignments.'

'In the dark? Okay, then. Good luck with that.'

Will grunted. He took the packet of Ginger Nuts. It felt lighter than he'd hoped. He held it up to the dim glow of the streetlight filtering into the cubby. Nearly empty. 'Okay,' he sighed. 'I guess we can give it a go.'

Pollo slapped Will on the knee. 'That's the spirit! What's the worst that can happen?'

Will opened his mouth, but Pollo interrupted. 'On second thoughts, don't answer that.'

CHAPTER EIGHTEEN

Under the cover of night, Benson shouldered through the door of the shed out back of the Royal Arms pub, his ears stinging with cold. It was too early yet for the drinkers in the front bar to be rowdy, for the jukebox to be cranking up — late enough, though, for the concrete floor to have lost what warmth it had scavenged from the day. He had a few precious hours to himself now at least. He was done with skulking on the edges of town, counting down the daylight.

He scanned the floor with his torch. Despite what the Duke had said about Tony's missus knowing about him, everything seemed to be where he'd left it — the hessian sacks he'd laid on the floor, his book, his backpack amongst the old paint cans. He flicked mouse droppings, fresh since leaving for the abattoir that morning, from the sacks, balanced his torch on his backpack and sat down.

He peeled back the lid of a tin of stew and shook its contents into his mouth, scraping out the last with his finger. Who had those voices in the playground cubbyhouse belonged to, he wondered. Delinquents-in-training sneaking something they'd nicked from a liquor cabinet? Maybe it was a couple of homeless kids. One morning last year, early, he'd gone fishing with his dad and seen two kids sleeping rough, rolled in a blanket on the dirt under a bridge. It hadn't looked like fun. If whoever was in the cubbyhouse was there again tomorrow night, he'd show them his shed.

Taking a grubby hoodie from his backpack, he lay down, bunching the hoodie under his head. He reached for his book, *Robinson Crusoe*. It was old, the story at least, written three centuries ago about a dude shipwrecked alone on an island — a bit like the *Cast Away* movie. The language was weird but you got used to it. His granddad had given it to him on his twelfth birthday, saying that the main character sure knew how to think for himself. It was lame alongside the Xbox Benson got from his parents, so he hadn't looked at it twice at the time. But he'd been going through some stuff not long ago and found it. And now he wished the old guy was around to chat about it with.

His iPod had run out of juice so there was no music to get lost in. It was just him and the book now, and trying to swap the stink of blood and guts that lingered in his nostrils with imaginings of beaches and hilltops; trying to believe in his heart that sometimes, like Crusoe, you had to do hard stuff in order to survive — that the deal he'd struck with the Duke was a necessary evil.

This time on a Saturday, he was usually in Kal's garage practising with the guys, Kal's little sister bopping in the corner and complaining when they repeated a snatch of song till they nailed it. Kal, his penniless mate. At the end of every session, Kal would carefully wipe down the strings of the old guitar he'd borrowed from Bixo and polish the thing till it shone.

Could what he and Kal had done be called a necessary evil too — if they hadn't got caught, if they'd gone ahead with it? Kal wanting something so badly, just that once; him trying to help out a mate in need? Whatever, it had all gone south. He'd been given his suspension and straightaway been packed off to Riddle Gully; then that girl had put that stuff in the newspaper, telling the world what a scumbag he was. The whole sloppy business had baked onto him somehow before he'd had a chance to put things right.

He couldn't go home, not now, not yet. He had something in common with Mr Crusoe. He was marooned ... in Princeville — a thief, a bad person, his very own shipwreck. And he could feel the tide rising, the water beginning to wet his feet. No music, no money, no phone, no bed, hungry, reeking and three days till payday. He flicked a daddy-long-legs off his page and lowered the book to his chest. He lay listening to the scuttling of cockroaches and the base *boom-boom* from the pub lounge. He cracked his knuckles one by one. He'd go back to the abattoir tonight 'cos he didn't know what else to do.

CHAPTER NINETEEN

Will and Pollo stood beneath the last streetlamp on the road out of town to the abattoir. Pollo held Shorn Connery by the head while Will, the end of a paintbrush to his chin, circled them slowly.

'Nearly done,' said Will. 'Just a dab ... here ... on his ear.'

'It doesn't have to be perfect, Will,' said Pollo. 'I'm freezing to death! Just so long as he looks more like a Dalmatian than a sheep! It's just a precaution.'

'A precaution against everything going wrong and Shorn Connery getting mixed up with his mates on Death Row.'

'The teeny-tiny possibility of things going wrong, Will! Stop being such a pessimist.'

'I still don't see why we have to bring him,' muttered Will.

'How else are we going to find Ear among five hundred head of sheep?'

'What if she doesn't recognise him now he's covered in spots?'

'We've been over this,' sighed Pollo. 'She will. Trust me.'

'Trust you?' Will touched up a blob on Shorn Connery's back. 'Look where that's got me.'

Pollo huffed and turned to Shorn Connery. 'Hold still, old buddy. It's for your own good. If anyone sees us we don't want you —'

'— to be turned into C-H-O-P-S!' giggled Will, to a glare from Pollo.

Baa-aa-aa-aah!

'We'll need to do something about that bleating of his, too,' said Will, adding a daub of black paint to Shorn Connery's nose.

Pollo leaned close to Shorn Connery and looked him in the eye. 'You'll have to be quiet as a mouse!' she whispered. 'You can do that, can't you?'

Baa-aa-aa-aah!

'Hmm,' said Will. 'What about this?' He stood and took a deep breath. *Woo-woo-woo-woof!*

Pollo swung around, sprawling onto her backside, her head spinning, searching.

Will grinned. 'Barking — it's my specialty. I used to sneak up and get Angela with it all the time. If Shorn Connery bleats at the wrong moment I can bark in sync with him!'

'It could come in handy!' said Pollo.

'Maybe,' said Will. He applied a final spot to Shorn Connery's tail. 'All done. We're good to go.'

'Brilliant!' Pollo helped Will shrug into his backpack, still loaded with Shorn Connery's fleece. With stippled clouds wisping across the moon, the girl, the boy and the oddly-shaped Dalmatian set off up the road.

*

Pollo, Will and Shorn Connery approached the abattoir through the ghostly moon-shadows of the avenue of eucalyptus trees. Pollo and Will tiptoed up a short flight of steps onto the unloading dock platform. From there, at sheep-truck height, a wooden ramp ran steeply down to the dirt of the holding pens next to the slaughterhouse. The closer pen was still empty — just a stretch of trampled sand and animal droppings. In the second pen, grey moonlight bounced off the backs of the huddled sheep. Somewhere unseen, the guard dog barked once, perhaps at an owl or a rat.

'Is it time?' whispered Pollo.

Will nodded and shouldered off his backpack. He unzipped it and brought out the tightly packed hessian bag containing Shorn Connery's fleece, sewn shut by Mr Mallard. Pollo flicked at the string with her pen-knife and the fleece sprang forth, surrounding their feet like overflowing soap suds. They eased it into two halves, its smooth lanolin greasing their fingers, the buttery smell of it filling their nostrils.

'You first,' said Will.

Pollo plunged both fists into one of the piles and draped it over her head and shoulders. 'How do I look?'

'Like a sheep that's had a very bad night's sleep.' Will pinched his nose, trying not to laugh.

'Now you,' said Pollo.

Will did the same. The fleece bunched over his head and spilled down his back.

'I'd give anything to have my camera with me right now!' chuckled Pollo. She picked up some scraps of wool from the platform. 'We should tuck these into our pockets. The more wool we've got on us, the more that guard dog will be thrown off our scent.'

When they finished they looked like a cross between giant chickens and Abominable Snowmen.

'We don't look much like sheep,' said Will.

'No, but we sure smell like them!'

Shorn Connery, resplendent in his spots, stared up at them, looking puzzled. *Baa-aa-aah!*

'Shsh!' said Pollo. 'It's only a loan, old buddy. As soon as we find Ear and get her out of here we'll —'

Meh-eh-eh!

Shorn Connery stood stiff, his ears pricked forward, sniffing the air. Pollo and Will looked at one another.

Baa-aa-aah!

Meh-eh-eh!

Suddenly Shorn Connery shot away. He clattered down the ramp and pelted across the empty expanse of the first pen, his rope lead bouncing behind him. Charging at full speed, he bounded high over the metal bars separating him from the next pen — and Ear. For a flash, Pollo and Will saw his spotty figure sailing in the moonlight, and then ... nothing. The mob of sheep made way for him, then closed together, engulfing him, making Shorn Connery — wherever he was — one of their own.

'He's meant to bring Ear to us!' cried Will. 'Not the other way round! Pollo, you said —'

'It doesn't matter now!' squeaked Pollo. 'Quick, we have to get after him!'

CHAPTER TWENTY

Pollo and Will slid and slipped down the stock ramp. Across the dirt of the empty holding pen they ran, their clothes stuffed with fleece, their cloaks flopping, the sheep in the pen ahead bleating and backing off as far as they could. As Pollo and Will climbed the bars of the second pen's fence, some sheep panicked, clambering over the other animals' backs with sprawling hooves.

Sitting atop the fence, shadows shifted as clouds rolled across the moon. Will and Pollo scanned the pen, straining to see Shorn Connery and his spots. But between the shadows and the tight scrum of sheep, they couldn't make out a single spot of him. From around the corner of the building, the guard dog began to bark. Between barks they heard its throaty growl.

Suddenly Will tugged on Pollo's arm. 'Look!' In

a room inside the building, a beam of torchlight was sweeping from side to side. 'Somebody's here! It must be a nightwatchman!'

'A nightwatchman!' cried Pollo. 'I don't want to put Shorn Connery's disguise to the test, Will! If the nightwatchman twigs to it, tomorrow Shorn Connery could be —'

This time, Will couldn't spell it, even to himself. Chops! He would never again be able to eat one, for fear it belonged to Shorn Connery. Meanwhile, Pollo was clambering down the other side of the railings, the fleece cape flowing around her shoulders. Will followed hastily, grabbing hold of the loop of Pollo's jeans just as the flock engulfed them. They crouched low, holding their fleeces tight around their necks. They shunted forward, searching for Shorn Connery. Sheep bayed and kicked and pressed in on them. Animal fear mingled with the damp stench kicked up by their hooves.

Inside, the torchlight was moving down a corridor, bouncing off the roof through the high, narrow windows. They heard the skitter of a dog's claws on concrete and a low growl.

Just then, Pollo caught a glimpse of what she was desperate to see — a spotted head. And in the flimsy light, another ear — black and twirling — beside it.

'Over there!' She pointed. 'In the corner! It's them! Oh dear ...'

Will peered and saw them too — and his heart sank. Shorn Connery and Ear were pressed into the farthest possible corner of the yard against the high fence arcing inward at the top — the fence that separated the sheep pens from the raised concrete platform next to the slaughterhouse. The two animals huddled together trembling, their ears flattened, as above them, only centimetres away behind the fence, crouched a brute of a dog — its eyes on Pollo and Will — quivering, slavering, its tongue glistening between its curved teeth.

'It can see us!' said Will.

'But it can't smell us!' said Pollo. 'It doesn't know what to bark at!'

They pressed forward into the mob of sheep, clumsy in their fleece-stuffed clothes and capes. Craning their necks to keep Shorn Connery and Ear in sight, they pushed into the swathe of animals till they stood panting in front of the two woolly lovebirds. Pollo flung herself at Shorn Connery and squeezed him with relief. At this, the dog hurled itself at the fence and bared its teeth even more, its purple gums rippling.

Over an exit door that opened onto the concrete platform, a blue security alarm began to flash. Shorn Connery and Ear snorted and shuffled fearfully, dodging Pollo's attempts to settle them. The dog gave a low growl, ready to start barking again.

'That dog's going to put the nightwatchman onto us!' hissed Will.

Pollo peered at the high steel fence. It would hold. It was worth a shot. Swallowing hard, she took a fistful of the thick fleece once sported by Shorn Connery and now draped across her shoulders. She faced the dog and slowly began flapping her arms.

The dog licked its lips and took a step backwards. Will followed Pollo's lead. The befuddled guard dog stopped snarling and sat back on its haunches, thrusting its nose in the air in short, puzzled jabs.

Pollo and Will stared at one another in disbelief. It had worked! An owl tooted softly in the distance; wind shuffled the leaves of the trees. They flapped their fleece-capes again. The dog stabbed its nose from side to side, flummoxed by the queer sheepy-human whiffs.

Inside the building, the torch beam was heading steadily for the nearby exit door. Whoever came through that exit would be almost face-to-face with Pollo and

Will in the enclosure below.

'They'll spot us straight off if they come out here,' cried Pollo. 'Keep flapping, Chicken Man! I'll try to rope up Ear and Shorn Connery.'

While Will flapped away at the confused guard dog, Pollo found the loose end of Shorn Connery's rope, slippery with sheep droppings, and tied it as best she could around Ear's neck. Light was trickling now through the gaps around the exit door onto the pavement. Someone rattled the door handle. The dog suddenly turned and hurtled along the concrete path to the door. It crouched in front of it, ears straining, hind legs twitching, ready to leap.

Pollo grabbed the middle of the rope. 'Let's get out of here!'

Pulling Shorn Connery and Ear, Will and Pollo shoved their way back through the squeeze of sheep, keeping low. They were nearly at the first fence — the empty pen on the other side and the unloading dock clear in the distance — when they heard the exit door clunk open. They snuck a backwards look over their shoulders. Through the opening, in the pulsing blue security light, they saw the half-silhouette of someone's head and shoulders.

The dog lurched at the gap between door and wall. But instead of calming the animal as a nightwatchman would, the person yelped and tried to pull shut the door. The animal leapt. The dog snarled, a cuff of trousers in its teeth. From behind the door the leg kicked madly, the dog's jaws locked around it, trying to drag the leg's owner outside.

'Something's not right,' whispered Pollo.

'Drop! Back! Get away! Go home!' It was a male voice. Young. Frightened. In the leaping beam of his flailing torch, Will and Pollo could now see his shoulder braced against the door, the peak of his cap catching the frame and tilting upward as the dog tried to drag him out. 'Let go! Stop!' he yelled.

'That cap ...' said Pollo.

'That voice ...' said Will.

'Benson!' They both sprang. Pollo dropped the rope tethering Shorn Connery and Ear. Bulky and cumbersome with fleece, they plunged back into the mob of sheep. They reached the high, curved, steel fence just as the dog pulled Benson by his leg outside onto the concrete path. Benson went down with a thud. The dog stood over him, snarling, its big paws across Benson's shoulders, ropes of saliva swinging from its jaws.

'Don't look it in the eye!' yelled Pollo to Benson. 'Try to curl up if you can!' She jammed the toe of her runner between the fence railings and began to climb. But with all the fleece inside and outside her clothing and the curve of the fence at the top, it was slow going. Now something was holding her back! She'd snagged on some wire. 'Will!' she yelled. 'I'm caught up! I can't get over!'

'Help!' screamed Benson. He rolled his head toward Will, safe on the other side of the fence. 'Please!'

Will was rigid like a statue. He'd never seen anyone in real trouble before. In real terror. It wasn't like TV — it was all around him and it didn't cut away to a hero who knew just what to do. He opened and shut his mouth, his eyes darting from Benson, to Pollo stuck on the fence, and back again.

The dog growled and stiffened. Somewhere deep inside Will, a switch quietly flicked. His brain cleared like he'd whiffed ammonia. He opened his mouth and suddenly, barely knowing what he was doing, he was barking like a mad dog himself. *Woo-woo-woo-woo-woo-woo-woo!* He did it again, his voice rising and cracking. *Woo-woo-woo-WOO-WOO-WOO-WOO!*

The dog stopped snarling and looked at Will —

this authoritative sheep-human creature with odd pronunciation. It cocked its head to one side, its hairy brow furrowed.

Woo-woo-woo-WOO-WOO-WOO-WOO! Will flapped his fleece as he barked. The animal whimpered and edged backwards, releasing Benson who scrambled back against the wall.

Pollo finally tore herself free and jumped backwards into the pen with Will. They waved their woollen capes. The dog stalked toward them suspiciously, its eyes fixed on them through the fence, its nose doing wheelies in the air. Benson took his chance and belted for the door.

'We've tripped the alarm! So disappear fast!' he yelled, the exit door banging shut behind him.

A second later, the door opened again a crack. 'Thanks!' The guard dog turned and pelted at him. Just in time, Benson slammed the door closed against its nose.

Pollo and Will looked at one another, breathing sharply, both wondering the same thing. What was Benson doing inside the abattoir at night? Had they found him too late to stop him sliding further into trouble? Or were they wrong about who Benson's 'true self' really was? There was no time to talk. They waded back into the mob of sheep, back toward the fence separating their pen from the empty one beside the unloading dock, to search for Shorn Connery and Ear all over again.

'Do you think he recognised us?' puffed Pollo.

'I reckon so,' said Will. 'He looked me right in the eye. By now he's probably halfway down the driveway with whatever it is he's nicked.'

'And whoever's coming to check that security alarm,' said Pollo, 'is probably halfway up.'

CHAPTER TWENTY-ONE

In the scant moonlight, Will and Pollo pushed through the murmuring sheep, expecting any second to hear a swarm of police cars revving up the narrow road to the abattoir.

'We've still got to cross that empty holding pen,' puffed Will. 'We'll stand out like emus in a chicken coop if they catch us there!'

'Let's concentrate on finding Shorn Connery and Ear first,' whispered Pollo. '*Then* we can panic. Keep your fleece on. It'll help disguise us.'

'Even if we do manage to find them, we have to get them both over the fence. That'll take forever!'

'One problem at a time, eh, Will?' said Pollo, ploughing on.

To their giant relief, the lovebirds hadn't strayed

far from where they had left them. They didn't seem to notice when Pollo grabbed the rope tying them together. Will and Pollo were huffing and puffing, trying to lift them over the railings, when they saw a figure, his cap on sideways, bounding toward them across the dirt on the other side of the fence. Pollo and Will swapped glances. Benson! And apart from his torch, he didn't look to be carrying anything!

'You two saved my bacon back there,' he puffed. He swung his legs and was soon sitting atop the fence. He shone the torch beam over their faces. 'You're the ones from Riddle Gully, aren't you? Fuzzball and Punk! Only you've both stacked on some pudding since I last saw you.'

Will patted his stomach. 'It's sheep's wool. We're wearing it inside our clothes too to cover our scent.'

'Smart thinking,' said Benson.

'It came from my faithful assistant, Shorn Connery here,' said Pollo. 'He helps in the strangest ways!'

'I reckon you got about three minutes before security gets here. I'll lend you a hand.'

He pocketed the torch and jumped down. Together they managed to get Shorn Connery and Ear over the railings and into the empty pen. The two sheep didn't need any encouragement. As soon as their hooves hit the ground they galloped hell-for-leather for the ramp rising to the loading dock. Pollo, holding their rope, had to sprint hard to keep from being pulled over.

They all rattled up the ramp — Shorn Connery, Ear, Pollo, Will and Benson. They had just jumped onto the unloading dock, their lungs burning, when through the trees they saw headlights sweeping into the abattoir turn-off from the main road. They grabbed Will's backpack where he'd left it by the ramp and ran for it. They reached the pools of deep shadow beneath the trees by the car park just as a four-wheel drive rumbled past and skidded to a halt. Two burly security guards leapt out, hands on truncheons at their hips.

The men strode up to the abattoir entrance, flashlights sweeping; Pollo, Will, Benson, Shorn Connery and Ear scurried away into the dark.

*

In the field alongside the access road, the troop followed the fence-line away from the abattoir, their feet groping through the dry twigs and prickly shrubs. No one dared to switch on a torch.

'Let's stop for a second to let our eyes adjust,' said Pollo. She closed her eyes.

'Do you want to stop and unstuff yourselves?' said Benson. 'It's not uncomfortable? You're not getting too hot?'

'You're kidding! It's the first time all day I've felt nice and toasty!' Pollo opened her eyes to see Benson rubbing his arms. 'Oh ... would *you* like some wool?'

'Wouldn't mind,' said Benson.

Pollo and Will each tugged out hanks and passed them over to Benson, who stuffed them down the front of his hoodie. He bobbed his head approvingly. 'Sweet!'

'Save some,' said Pollo. 'Just in case.'

'In case what?' said Will.

'Those security guards will have to come back this way,' said Pollo. 'We might have to hide again.'

'They won't have found anything wrong,' said Benson. 'I didn't nick anything; I didn't damage anything.'

'You didn't?' said Will. He added hastily, 'Not that I'm surprised or anything.'

'If you don't mind me asking, Benson, what *were* you doing at the abattoir tonight?' said Pollo.

'Hah! Matter of fact, I do mind. You don't think I couldn't ask the same thing about you two?'

'Aah, it's the heart-rending tale of two sheep who

fell in love,' said Will with a giggle. He pointed at Ear who was bustling ahead alongside Shorn Connery. 'We wanted to rescue this one with the black ear from getting the chop.'

'We were looking for you at the abattoir — this afternoon anyway,' said Pollo.

'What? So you could write another rubbish story about me and bury me in an even deeper hole?'

'No,' said Pollo. 'So that we — I — could apologise. I had no business saying that stuff about you in the newspaper. Even if it had been true it wouldn't have been right.'

'Whaddya mean, "even if it had been true"?' said Benson.

'The real thief was a raven,' said Will. 'At least we're pretty certain it was — we haven't checked for sure because its nest is too high to climb up to.'

'A raven?' said Benson. 'Like ... you mean ... a crow?'

'Uh-huh, except that ravens have those dangly throat feathers,' said Pollo, 'and when they caw they sound kinda sad. Anyway, this one's got a funny feather sticking out on its shoulder. It's been stealing things to decorate its nest.'

'When we found out you'd nicked stuff at school,'

said Will, 'we got it in our heads you were heaps worse than you really are.'

'Gee, thanks, Punk,' said Benson.

'I'm sorry, Benson,' said Pollo. 'What I did was really wrong. It was lazy investigating, bad reporting, and it put you into all sorts of trouble.'

'S'okay,' said Benson. 'I couldn't stand it at my uncle's anyway.' He walked on a few paces then added, 'And I didn't help much — the way I reacted at the cemetery. I got a bit freaked-out, knowing Punk's stepdad was a cop.'

'So you *were* eavesdropping on us at the rollercoaster that day!' said Pollo.

'Well, yeah. When I heard you say he was a cop, I wondered if the cops in Riddle Gully knew about my suspension too.'

'HB never said anything if he did,' said Will.

'Why were you crouching behind the tent stalls later on, though?' said Pollo. 'It keeps bugging me. You sure looked like you were up to no good.'

Benson laughed wryly. 'I was hiding from my uncle! He was wanting me to take photos of him winning that stupid chutney contest. They hadn't even announced the results yet! He's such a creep. I didn't want the whole town knowing we were related.'

'I guess I kind of ruined that for you,' said Pollo.

'They would've found out sooner or later.'

'Hiding from Mayor Bullock,' murmured Will. 'We should have thought of that, eh, Pollo?'

'Yes, Will. We should have.'

They trudged beside the fence, the peppery scent of coming rain in their nostrils, wind snipping about their ears, their runners crunching on the sticks and curled bark sloughed off by the trees. They'd been quiet for several minutes when Benson spoke.

'I'm not a thief, ya know,' he said. 'I can't blame the school for suspending me, but I'm not just some scumbag who steals things for kicks.'

Will and Pollo tried to read one another's faces in the darkness. Was this Benson's old self trying to find its feet again?

'So ... just checking,' said Will. 'You're not a thief deep down, or you're not a thief full stop?'

'Full stop.'

They shuffled a few more paces. 'Why did your school suspend you, then?' asked Pollo.

'It's complicated,' said Benson.

'We're pretty good at "complicated",' said Will.

Benson stopped. He turned to Will and Pollo. 'What would you two know about complicated?' he snorted. 'Listen, I know you guys mean well, but no way am I ever telling you my personal stuff. People's secrets aren't just for fun. They're not for collecting like footie cards.'

'And now *you* listen, Buttface!' said Will, blood suddenly rushing to his temples and angry words to his tongue. He caught the sensation by the tail and took ten deep, slow breaths. Benson kept quiet, curious. Feeling steadier, Will continued. 'You don't know what's going on in our lives any more than we know what's going on in yours. You're not the only one in the world with problems.'

'You saying you got problems?' scoffed Benson. 'Proper ones? Yeah, pull the other one, Punk.'

Will thought of Pollo, whose mum had died when she was little, too soon to leave her with proper memories even. He thought of the graffiti mess he'd got himself into last summer, and of his dad, Clive, who went on about father-and-son bonding but had forgotten to do much about it since the rug rat came along. But Benson Bragg didn't need to hear any of that.

'Problems are problems,' said Will. 'It's not like some count and some don't — and it sure isn't for *you* to decide. *You* don't get to give 'em a score out of ten, Benson Bragg. All that counts is that people know what to do with their problems. Maybe we can get rid of them if we're lucky. But maybe we just have to say "Hey, you know what? I can live with that." You fix 'em or you learn to get along with 'em. Just don't go round acting stupid and feeling sorry for yourself!'

Will stood facing Benson, one fist wrapped around his cloak of wool, hoping it might hide his trembling from the older boy in the sudden shaft of moonlight.

'Man! You say some sharp stuff for a little dude,' said Benson. 'I've never thought of getting along with a problem before.' He swatted Will on the side of his head and smiled. 'Thanks, Punk. I'll keep it in mind.'

At that moment, they heard a vehicle bumping down the road from the abattoir, its high-beam headlights bouncing. Pollo and Benson darted behind a wide tree trunk, crouched low and pulled wool over their heads. Will hurled his backpack into the low branches of a bush and jammed his head in after it.

The four-wheel drive passed. No one moved for a long time. Even Shorn Connery and Ear grazed quietly, obscured by bushes. Eventually Pollo, Will and Benson heard the shift of gears as the car accelerated up the main road back towards Princeville. Only the night crickets and the mob of sheep bleating in the distant holding pen could be heard.

Will whispered from within a snare of spiky foliage. 'Is it safe to come out?'

'Yeah, probably,' said two voices. He edged backside-first from his hiding spot and turned to see Pollo and Benson pointing at him from either side of their tree, their shoulders juddering trying not to laugh.

'Can't be too careful,' said Will, straightening up and chasing a crawler off his neck.

CHAPTER TWENTY-TWO

After walking through the back streets of sleeping Princeville, they had reached an intersection where the wind whipping off the black ocean was so cold it felt like a slap.

'Well, this is where we part,' said Benson, pulling his hoodie over his head, cap and all. 'I dunno what you guys are doing, but my castle is along that-a-way.' He pointed up the road where moonlight glinted blue from the tin rooftops and the dead street lamps. 'It's been a swell evening. We should do it again sometime.'

'But you're not staying in Princeville, are you?' cried Pollo. 'You're coming home with us, aren't you — back to Riddle Gully?'

'Why would I do that?' said Benson. 'Why would I go back to where everyone thinks I'm a scumbag? Where my uncle takes it out on my gran every time I breathe in when he thinks I should be breathing out?' Benson kicked a pebble on the road. It ricocheted off the kerb and bounced out of earshot.

'But we'll make sure everyone knows you're not a scumbag,' said Pollo. 'You can't stay here,' said Pollo. 'Those workers at the abattoir ...'

'Some of 'em are okay,' said Benson. He began to walk in the direction of the Royal Arms.

'Benson, I have to know,' called Pollo, 'because I started all this and I don't want you to get into more trouble ...' She hurried after him and grabbed his jacket. 'Why *were* you at the abattoir tonight? It's something to do with that man who drove you home, isn't it?' she said. 'He put you up to something, didn't he?'

Benson stopped. He looked up at the clouds scudding across the stars, his hands shoved into his pockets. 'I guess I can tell you — it's not like I went through with it.' He sighed. 'That man you saw me talking with is the top dog out there. The Duke, they call him. I was meant to steal the boss's family photo and any cash I could find — like some kind of initiation. They talked about it like it was just a bit of fun, a prank. But when I got in there, I couldn't do it.'

'Because you're not a thief,' said Pollo.

'Yeah,' said Benson, 'but also because I didn't want them to own me.'

'Own you, like in having something they could blackmail you with?' said Pollo.

'Nah,' said Benson. 'More like making me do something I thought was dead wrong. Putting a dent in the kind of person I want to be.' Benson looked down at the footpath and kicked another stone. 'Sounds crazy, eh?'

'Sounds like the un-craziest thing I've ever heard,' said Pollo.

'I'm with you,' said Will.

'I mean, I'm standing there, looking at the boss's wife and kids all smiling in the photo, and suddenly I don't give a toss whether the Duke lets me into the group or not. So I leg it. I was trying to get out of there when that guard dog came at me. Dunno what the Duke and his mates will do to me tomorrow.'

'Who cares?' said Pollo. 'You stood up to them. You should be proud of yourself.'

'Easy for you to say, Fuzzball.'

'You know,' said Will, 'there's a chance they might respect you for it.'

'Maybe,' said Benson. He took a sharp, deep breath. 'I'll stick it out here till payday, anyway. Then I'll have enough to catch the bus home.'

'You don't have to stay in Princeville,' said Will. 'I can lend you the bus fare back to the city.'

'I'm not a thief and I'm not a sponger either,' said Benson, his voice cracking.

'I know what you are, though,' said Pollo, springing in front of Benson and thrusting her face near his. 'You're proud! Instead of accepting our help, you want to risk getting into more strife and have everyone go on treating you like you're a bad person.' She stamped her foot. 'Come back to Riddle Gully with us! Prove to everyone you're not what they think you are.'

'I don't have to prove anything to anyone!' said Benson.

'Then prove it to yourself,' said Pollo. 'Stop acting like a fugitive and running close to trouble.'

Benson folded his arms. 'Even if I did go back to Riddle Gully, how am I meant to prove I didn't nick anything anyway?' He looked at Pollo. 'People won't just take your word for it.'

'That's easy!' said Will. 'Get up that tree and look inside that ravens' nest.'

'What if you two are wrong? What if the only things in that nest are baby ravens?'

'Then you'll be no worse off than now,' said Pollo. 'We lend you the fare home and you pay us back sometime.'

'You've only got your old self to lose,' added Will.

'My what?'

'Your old self,' said Will. 'The kid you want to be, like you said before — not this thief-person you're acting like, that everyone's treating you like.'

'Plus, you can get your mobile back from your uncle!' said Pollo, suddenly remembering the conversation on Mayor Bullock's doorstep.

Benson's eyes lit up. 'My phone? Why didn't you mention that before?'

They laughed, hunching into the squalling wind. 'Come on,' said Will. He pointed up the street toward the playground. '*Our* castle's this-a-way — and there's room for three.'

CHAPTER TWENTY-THREE

They huddled in the cubbyhouse in a pile of fleece, Benson's torch hanging on a loose nail, its beam shining and shadowing their faces. Wind keened through the gaps and knotholes in the wooden planks. A hundred metres away, the ocean pounded the shore. Benson, his head lowered, was talking.

'His name's Kal. He's my best mate. We've got a garage band — borrowed gear and stuff. His family has trouble making ends meet, even though they work really hard. Kal hasn't got a cent to scratch himself with — gives it all to his family. He's only got a phone 'cos the boss where he works Friday and Saturday nights gave him one when he found out Kal was walking home after midnight.

'So the music camp at school is coming up — three

days in the hills somewhere — and aside from the fact that Kal plays lead guitar like it's wired straight into his brain, he's fallen like a sack of spuds for this girl who plays cello. Kal wanted to go on that music camp like crazy. But there was the money, see. It cost more than he earns in a month.

'So this girl in English is bragging about how much she's made on-selling jewellery at school — stuff she's bought on the internet. And she shows everyone her fat shiny wallet. Meanwhile Kal's down in the dumps 'cos the money for music camp has to be in that day. So me and Kal are walking to Maths. We go past the library and on the rack outside is this girl's bag — you can tell it's hers by all the little teddy bears and stuff dangling off it. Sheesh! It's not even zipped up. So I make this smart-alec joke about the answer to all Kal's problems being right there. Funny, huh?'

Benson winced. 'I think I was joking but, looking back, maybe part of me wasn't. I dunno.' He was silent a while before continuing. 'Anyway, I keep walking and ... next thing I know Kal's next to me, opening his bag and showing me. He's got it — her wallet. It's just sitting there on top of his books. And he's white and sweating.

'I grab the stupid wallet and talk some sense into

him, and we're about to put it back. But right then the principal comes round the corner so, course, I chuck it into Kal's open bag. But she must have seen. She checks our bags and when she holds up the wallet, I dunno, I just blurt out that it's mine, I took it. And I stick to my story —' Benson looked at Pollo and Will, '— until now. Hell, it was my fault, wasn't it? I gave him the idea. And I figured Kal needed a break — I've got things so much easier than him. So the principal did what she had to do. She suspended me, "effective Monday".'

'What did Kal do?' asked Pollo.

'He tried to tell everyone it was him who'd taken it, not me. I heard on the grapevine he apologised to the girl. That must've taken some guts. But Kal's the kind of soft-spoken dude no one listens to much. Talks more through his music than conversation. His mum and dad thought he was wanting to get suspended so's we could hang out together.'

'So neither of you went on music camp,' said Will.

'Nup,' said Benson. 'It was last week.'

'And now everyone thinks you're a thief,' said Will.

'Everyone except Kal — and maybe Mum and Gran.'

'And us,' added Will and Pollo.

They listened to the gusts of wind outside and

hunched under the fleece against the splinters of rain pushing through the cracks. Will found the Ginger Nut packet and felt its ridges. Two left. He passed the packet to Benson who ripped the wrapper and, one after the other, popped both biscuits into his mouth. Will's eyes widened.

'Sorry,' said Benson, his cheeks bulging, 'did you want one?'

'No, no!' said Will, cradling the wrapper tenderly and salvaging the corner crumbs with a licked finger. 'You go right ahead. Plenty more where they came from ... in the shop.'

'Thanks,' Benson mumbled through his mouthful.

'You know,' said Pollo after a moment, 'maybe it doesn't matter what you did or didn't do at school so much as how you feel about it now.'

'What are you getting at?' said Benson.

'Well, you and Kal are both really sorry for what happened, right?' said Pollo. 'And you two have a garage band, right?'

'Yeah ... go on.'

'Well, maybe you could give a Sorry concert.'

'A Sorry concert ...' said Benson. 'To, like, tell everyone we're sorry for what we did?'

'That's the general idea,' said Pollo.

'And that we'd like to make up for it,' Benson added, nodding slowly.

'And I guess,' chipped in Will, 'that when everyone comes along and has a good time, it's their way of saying, "Hey, we all make mistakes, we forgive you, let's start over". I've gotta say, the times I've decided to forgive and forget, it's been a load off.'

'Yeah, I've been there,' said Benson.

'Like I forgive you for taking the last Ginger Nut,' grinned Will, ducking a cuff from Benson.

'I've got it!' cried Pollo. 'You could make it a benefit concert and give the money you raise to a good cause.'

Benson sat forward. 'After the last few nights, I wouldn't mind helping out homeless people,' he said quietly.

'People who have to sleep in playground cubbyhouses every night,' said Will.

'Or clapped-out sheds behind pubs.'

'I can help with publicity,' said Pollo, her mind whirring. 'What's your band called?'

Benson shrugged. 'We haven't got a name. We've never needed one.' His eyes twinkled in a grin. 'How about The Ravens?'

They all laughed. 'The Ravens,' said Will. 'That's neat! If you want, I can design your logo for you.'

'I can see the headline now,' said Pollo. 'Riddle Gully Link to Homeless Benefit; Concert Dubbed a "Raven" Success!'

'It could work,' said Benson. 'It'd be scary, but it could work.' He leaned back against the wall, a smile spreading across his face, his head bobbing to a rhythm only he could hear.

*

A dirty grey light was spilling over the playground when Shorn Connery and Ear's bleating drew Pollo, Will and Benson from the cubbyhouse. The three groaned and stretched, bits of Shorn Connery's wriggly fleece clinging to their clothes and their sticky hair. The air was cold and still. Seaweed was massed on the beach in dark shoals, its sulphurous smell wafting on the air. The sea looked sullen but exhausted. On the horizon, shafts of sun burned the rims of the clouds.

Shorn Connery and Ear stood side by side a few metres away, roped to the dew-covered seesaw.

Baa-aa-aah!

Meh-eh-eh!

They fixed the three humans with glassy stares,

blinking their stiff white eyelashes. Buttoning the jacket she'd borrowed from Will snugly around her neck, Pollo walked across and scratched Shorn Connery's nose. 'Good morning, old buddy! Morning, Ear! Thanks for the alarm call! What would we do without you?'

Benson looked up from the water fountain where he was slurping from a cupped hand. 'Sleep in maybe?'

'H-how long d'you reckon we'll h-have to w-wait till a ute c-comes along?' said Will, his teeth chattering.

'Farmers get going pretty early,' said Pollo. 'And if a farmer doesn't come, there's always the bus.'

Benson pointed at Shorn Connery and Ear. 'Get real! No way am I getting on a bus with those two!'

'H-hanging out with P-pollo, you f-find yourself d-doing a lot of s-stuff you don't ex-p-pect.' Will jogged on the spot, his hands tucked into his armpits.

'I'm just kidding,' laughed Pollo. 'Give us your phone, eh, Will. I think it's time to call Dad.'

'But he's m-miles away at that w-wedding, isn't he?'

'Miles away from Riddle Gully maybe,' said Pollo, 'but only just down the road from Princeville.'

'W-what? You mean, while we were ch-chasing sheep and f-fighting dogs and f-freezing our ch-cheeks off, he was ... r-roast beef ... p-pavlova ... w-warm?'

'Don't forget wedding cake,' said Pollo.

'And scoffing w-wedding cake! He was f-five minutes up the r-road the whole t-time?'

'More like ten,' said Pollo. 'But I don't know why you're squeaking, Will. Firstly, like I said before, I could hardly ask him to spoil his first real date since I can remember. He might not go on another one for ten years. And Wanda, his lady-friend, would have had to come too because he drove her to the wedding. Secondly, we weren't expecting to find Benson till morning, remember? We *had* to stay here. Toughen up! What's a night outdoors in lovely spring weather like this?'

Will opened his mouth to argue then shut it again. He dug his phone from a pocket and handed it to Pollo, looking out over the grey ocean and the misty cloudbank bringing a rainshower their way. 'I just want a b-big, hot p-pie.'

'I'm with you there, Punk,' said Benson. 'But make it two.'

CHAPTER TWENTY-FOUR

Shorn Connery, Ear, Will, Benson and Pollo stuffed themselves into the back of Joe di Nozi's four-wheel drive. Far from being tetchy about his daughter's surprise phone call at six in the morning, Pollo's father had seemed almost cheerful at the prospect of checking out early from his motel. Wanda sat in the front seat looking out the side window, her lips pressed together, a horizontal finger sealing her nostrils. She hadn't seemed at all pleased to meet any of them.

'The land looks beaut in the morning mist, don't you think, Wanda?' said Joe hopefully as they rolled along. 'Your cats will be glad to see you home early, I'll bet. Hope you don't mind clearing up this business in Riddle Gully on the way. It takes seventy-odd k's off the trip.'

Wanda lifted her finger from under her nose. 'The

sooner you get rid of ... I mean, drop off this lot, the better.' Her finger resumed its position.

'Excellent. Right.' said Joe, tapping his fingers on the steering wheel and rustling up a tune to hum.

'So, how was the wedding?' asked Pollo.

'Terrific!' said Joe. 'The band had everyone up dancing!' He glanced sideways at Wanda. 'Well, nearly everyone.'

'If you could call it dancing,' said Wanda. 'That kind of music always gives me a throbbing headache — all that rhythm. And the beef was tough, didn't you think, Joe?'

'Me? Can't say I noticed,' said Joe. 'My bit was nice.'

'Tough *and* oversalted,' said Wanda.

Pollo studied Wanda from the back seat. She hadn't picked it up on the dating service photos but, seeing her now, it was as plain as day. Wanda was beige — beige hair, beige skin, beige lipstick, beige jumper and jeans, even the toenails in her high-heeled beige sandals. In fact — Pollo swung around to check — she looked quite a bit like Shorn Connery. But worst of all, Wanda acted beige. *I'll oversalt you,* thought Pollo, her mind running over the other ladies she and Sherri had seen on her dad's dating site.

Benson interrupted her sabotaging train of thought. 'This tree with the ravens' nest in it — how high is it? If you guys couldn't climb it, how am I meant to?'

'Perhaps we could tape a bunch of long poles together and tie a mirror to the top,' said Will. 'Then we could see inside the nest.'

'As long as we tied a whole lot of magnifying glasses underneath the mirror so we could see what it reflected,' said Pollo.

'A fire truck?' said Pollo's father over his shoulder.

'HB says they're for emergencies only, especially on weekends,' said Will.

'Fire trucks aren't the only things with long ladders,' said Benson. 'The rollercoaster guys use 'em too. The one we had at the Riddle Gully fair broke, though, and we had to borrow one from a window cleaner.'

Pollo and Will looked at one another. 'Mr Squeaky!' they yelled.

As they trundled along the highway towards Riddle Gully, Will rang Angela who called Mr Squeaky the window cleaner — and said she'd speak to Will later as to why he was gallivanting around the countryside instead of going to Canberra.

Benson then rang his mum in hospital who rang

her brother, the mayor, to tell him he'd been sacked as Benson's temporary guardian.

And Pollo rang Sherri. 'Drop everything and meet us at the car park near the cemetery!' she shouted into the phone. 'And bring a camera! Oh ... and Benson's gran!' She hung up, then quickly redialled. 'Please!' she added, and hung up again.

'I hope you're right about this,' said Benson, as they drove down the hill on the outskirts of town, the fields, the cemetery and the adjacent low hills and forest spreading ahead of them.

'We will be,' said Will. 'I'll bet you ten games of Monster Mash!'

Twenty minutes later, as Joe di Nozi's car bumped up to the cemetery gates, there was quite a mob there to welcome them — Benson's gran, Sherri, Angela, HB and, best of all, a sprightly fellow in blue overalls who, as Riddle Gully's window cleaner, boasted the longest ladder in the district. They all piled out of the car, except for Wanda, who said she prefer not to ruin her sandals, thank you all the same. Off to one side, Mayor Bullock leaned against his big black sedan, hands on his hips, scowling at his good-for-nothing nephew hugging his grandmother. Shorn Connery and Ear galloped away to

Shorn Connery's favourite lupin patch, kicking up clods of dewy grass.

Mr Squeaky sprang forward. 'I hear you young'uns are in urgent need of a set of rungs. People want a ladder, they straight off think fire truck, when they should be thinking Mr Squeaky!' He handed a business card to Pollo. 'In case you want to write something in the newspaper,' he said with a wink. Pollo read the card — *Mr Squeaky's Window Washing. Squeaky Clean or Your Money Back. No Job Too Small or Too High* — and tucked it in her pocket. You never knew when a long ladder might come in handy.

Everyone except Wanda and Mayor Bullock helped unload Mr Squeaky's longest extendable ladder. Arms hooked over it, they marched like a giant centipede through the cemetery, Mayor Bullock trailing grudgingly behind. They passed Mrs Turner's grave and crossed the meadow to the forest near the head of the Diamond Jack hiking trail, where the giant red gum spread its knotty branches.

They could hear the ravens cawing as they approached. *Arp-arp-aaah!*

The group leaned the ladder against the gnarly trunk and Mr Squeaky tested its hold. It locked firmly.

'Up you go, Benson,' said Pollo.

Benson quietly shook his head. 'But what if ...' He looked from Pollo to Will. 'One of you should go.'

From above, they heard the *whoosh-whoosh-whoosh* of wings as the ravens took to the sky.

'Whoever goes, we'd better be quick,' said Will. 'We don't want to disturb their nest any longer than we have to.'

'Okay,' mumbled Benson. 'I guess I'll go. Like you say, nothing to lose.'

He had just hoisted himself onto the first rung, when Pollo shouted to him. 'Wait! We need evidence!' She grabbed the camera from Sherri and passed it up to Benson. 'Good luck!' she whispered.

Nine heads craned as Benson climbed one rung at a time up the ladder. He pulled himself onto the branch and edged along it till he reached the untidy clump of woven sticks, bark, grasses and odds and ends that formed the ravens' nest. For a long time he sat there, quiet as a ghost, on the branch staring out across the cemetery, unable to look inside.

On the ground, Mayor Bullock shuffled impatiently. Everyone else watched Benson in the tree, so breathless and silent you could hear seeds splitting.

'This is a lot of hoo-ha!' Mayor Bullock snorted. 'A ruddy waste of —' But the chorus of *shshshsh*! was so fierce he shut his mouth.

Benson looked at the people below who had faith in him; at his gran waving her skinny arms, giving him a double thumbs up. He leaned sideways over the nest ... and saw the soft plant and animal fluff, tufts of his uncle's toupée, an old cat collar and glints of the gold and silver jewellery amongst which three speckled ravens' eggs nestled. He smiled, feeling the return from a hiding place deep inside of a weary friend — his old self, the person he wanted to be, the person he knew he was.

EPILOGUE

In the silvery dusk, Shorn Connery and Ear grazed peacefully behind Mrs Turner's tombstone. Pollo sat on the granite base, half reading a book, half watching the bats from the forest flitting over the cemetery meadow and listening to the ravens bedding down for the night. Suddenly she heard thudding footsteps. She turned to see Will running toward her, waving his mobile.

'Lucky we bought tickets!' he panted. 'We just got a text from Benson!'

Pollo took the phone, her smile widening as she read:

> Hey Fuzzball & Punk. Life is one scary rollercoaster. Tickets sold out with 3 days to go! Heap $$$ raised already. RAVENS ROCK!!! (and so do you.)

THE END

ACKNOWLEDGEMENTS

My thanks in the first instance go to Mitch Hart, Clinical Psychologist, for his generous advice on 'acceptance and commitment therapy' (ACT), the precepts of which gave shape to the theme of the novel brewing in my mind. Thank you also to Professor Van Ikin for his invaluable feedback on the initial draft; and to Gail Spiers for her friendship and endless support which, once again, extended to sharing her deep expertise in creating inspiring curriculum-linked teaching notes. Thank you to the team that is Fremantle Press — in particular Children's Publisher Cate Sutherland, Clive Newman and Claire Miller – for their continued guidance, professional support and faith. Lastly I thank my lively, loving family, especially my mother Margaret Everingham, my helpful and most loyal fan, and husband Dennis, my best bud.

— JB

JEN BANYARD

Jen Banyard is a Western Australian author. *Riddle Gully Runaway* is her third novel, following *Spider Lies* (2009) and *Mystery at Riddle Gully* (2012), both published by Fremantle Press. Jen attended Mount Pleasant Primary and Applecross High schools, and has a PhD in creative writing from the University of Western Australia. Fortunately she has never grown up.

ALSO BY JEN BANYARD

Another great Pollo di Nozi mystery.